AZALEA TRAIL

OF

DEATH

The Possumwood Mysteries Book 3

HOLLY DEY

Acknowledgements

I couldn't do this without the love and support of my wonderful family. I love you so much!

Chapter 1

PRIMROSE CORVINA DONOVAN would rather have been investigating a decomposing body than what she was about to do. PC, as she preferred to be called, sat in her car in front of the Possumwood Police Department, collecting her composure. Even though she had just solved the case of the Valentine's Brunch massacre, she was pretty sure that Chief Wilson—Woody, as she'd always known him—was not at all happy with her meddling in police business. Didn't matter at all that she had worked twenty-five years in Houston Homicide before she'd retired.

Can't sit out here all day.

March hadn't exactly blown in like a lion. It was 75 degrees and sunny, and it seemed like exactly the wrong kind of day for a trip to the metaphorical gallows. Possumwood PD wasn't big enough to have both a desk sergeant and a dispatcher, so whoever was on dispatch duty was also the receptionist.

"Hey, PC!" the young woman at the front desk chirped. "Happy Tuesday!"

"Hey, Annie. I haven't had a chance to say congratulations. Let's see." PC held out her hand in a come here gesture.

Annie beamed as she held up her left hand, the diamond engagement ring sparkling under the fluorescent light.

"That's gorgeous."

A door squeaked open, and Chief Elwood Wilson poked his head out. "Tran's a lucky man. Come into my office, Donovan."

Here we go. "Sure."

Woody gestured toward a chair that had seen better days, and he sat behind his own desk in a faux leather executive chair. Then he leaned forward, crossing his arms and propping his elbows on the battered desk. His hair was still mostly blue-black, although grey had crept in around the temples.

"Your mama's good?" he asked. The question sounded more perfunctory than genuine.

"Yeah. Her hip replacement is healing up pretty well."

"Glad to hear that. Now, since you've been back in Possumwood, you can't seem to keep your nose out of police business."

"Force of habit, I suppose." PC studied his face, but it was inscrutable.

"We don't get very many homicides, and most of those involve cheap whiskey, bad tempers, and a bar full of witnesses." Woody pushed away from the desk. The chair creaked in protest as he leaned back. "We do, however, participate in a regional cold-case coalition. We can probably find you a desk, if you find you cannot keep a leash on your curiosity."

What? "This isn't quite what I expected."

Woody's lips curled momentarily into a tiny smile. "It's mostly volunteer. But sometimes there are rewards offered for evidence that results in a conviction."

PC opened her mouth, then closed it again.

"I will tell you flat out—I don't have the budget to hire a full-time detective. But it might be that we, on rare occasions, would have need of a consultant."

She relaxed back into her chair. "Keep your friends close, but your enemies closer?"

Woody shrugged. "Why don't you pick a day and come in once a week or so and pick through the cold cases?"

"Why do I have the feeling there's an ulterior motive involved?" When she first arrived in Possumwood, someone had left the murder book from her father's unsolved case in her car. Was this connected in any way to Woody's cold case coalition? Did he even know about it?

Woody sat up straight. "Like what?"

"I don't know, exactly." PC stood up. "But I'll be in around ten on Thursday. Next week." She turned and left before he could reply.

What have I gotten myself into this time?

"No, Mama. I am not wearing a garden party hat." PC glared at the frivolous confection of a bonnet that lay in a pool of silk flowers and tulle on the kitchen table. "It looks ridiculous enough on its own. Look at me. What am I wearing?"

She gestured to her polo shirt and khakis.

"But honey, it's outside, and you're so fair complected." Rose pouted.

"Mama, it's March. And I have sunscreen. I'm not wearing that absurd hat. I'm happy to spend my Saturday with you, but not in that monstrosity. Besides, if we're going to pick up Justice and meet up with Daisy and Imogene for the tour, we need to have left five minutes ago. Have you got the tickets?"

"Of course, I do." Rose sighed and turned toward the front door. "Don't come crying to me for aloe vera when your nose blisters."

"I won't."

PC held the door for her mother. She was getting along pretty well without her cane, but PC thought they should bring it, just in case. She tucked it into the backseat, out of their way.

They arrived at the courthouse and PC found her sister, Daisy, and Rose's friend, Imogene, with about two minutes to spare. Rose passed out the tickets, programs, and pink wrist bands to her covey of tour takers.

A woman dressed like a southern belle—hoop skirt, acres of ruffles, and a lacy parasol—stood on the top step of the main entrance to the ornate county courthouse.

"Good mornin'! My name is Dinah Mae Brown, and I want to thank you all for comin' out to support the Mirabella County Historical Society on the first weekend of our annual Azalea Trail. Feel free to take as many pictures as you like outside the historical homes, but please refrain from photographing the inside, unless you ask the owner, of course, and they give you permission. One of our volunteers will be on hand to tell you the history of the house and answer any questions you may have." She patted some perspiration off her forehead and continued. "After our tour, refreshments in the rose garden at Happily Ever Afters are included with your ticket. Your wristband is your admission. Now, if y'all'll follow me?"

March weather on the Texas Coastal Plain is always a crap shoot. It may be 45° with a fresh wind that cuts through a body like a glass knife, or it may be 85° and so muggy breathing the air is like inhaling soup. And they might occur on consecutive days. A cold front had swept in during the night and dropped the mercury on the sweltering heat of the past two days. Today was one of those cool, sunny days that most people think about when they hear the word 'spring.'

Azaleas, from the palest pink to the darkest magenta, and everything in between, outlined the courthouse and brightened the shade of the surrounding live oaks. This was a plant that had nothing else in the world to do but bloom its heart out in early spring. That's it. Not another thing was expected from this otherwise nondescript bush. It was just as well they weren't fragrant—with so many flowers, the perfume would be enough to stun a mule.

Two things that go together, like a hand and a glove, a horse and a carriage, are azaleas and live oaks. Another match made in heaven, or hell, as the case may be: spring and oak pollen. While most deciduous trees drop a palette of fire-colored leaves in the fall, sneaky Texas live oaks wait until February or March. Olive-green catkins sprout at the same time as new olive-green foliage, evicting last year's leaves in a deluge of brown, oval confetti. Ripening catkins expel pollen until everything within spitting distance of the tree takes on a greenish-yellow coat. PC started to sniffle under this micro-granular assault.

The detective, who was the second youngest in the group, stayed at Rose's side, constantly assessing her condition. Growing up in Possumwood, she'd heard most of the stories about the historical homes. Pollen notwithstanding, she was just happy to be out in the fresh air and sunshine. She took a few pictures as they walked from house to house—perhaps she'd try painting azaleas later. So far, most of the homes had featured pink azaleas, but one had red and orange blossoms, and the mounds of flowers made her think of flames licking the front of the house as they were stirred by the gentle breeze.

Finally, they came upon the last house, the one PC had been waiting for. Its original owner had named the place Robinwood. The Greek Revival-style house featured snowy white flowers, massed around the back of a small pond with a gentle waterfall. A large goldfish rose to the surface, then darted back into the dark pool. Once the docent had finished her mini-lecture, the door opened and Drew Burlesconi appeared on the porch, framed by fluted white columns.

PC was so stunned by his outfit, she almost wished she'd worn the frilly hat Rose had tried to palm off on her. Drew wore a white pinstripe shirt and purple jacquard vest underneath an unbuttoned embroidered frock coat that grazed the tops of his knees. Squared-toed boots peeked out from under the hem of his black pinstripe trousers. Around his neck was an elaborately tied cravat, and his hair was pomaded into submission and slicked back.

He'd told her at their weekly darts game this past Wednesday that the historical society had brought him a get-up to wear, but he resolutely kept the details secret. She hadn't thought he'd go all out with the costume, but she was really impressed. The crazy bonnet Rose gave her this morning was half-hearted by comparison.

The tourists filed in through Drew's front door.

"You look amazing," she said as she passed.

He doffed an imaginary hat. A dozen or so history buffs roamed the first floor of the house. PC tried to make her way over to Drew, but one tour-taker after another stopped to chat with him. She could hardly blame them—he looked so dashing, in a Regency kind of way.

A patinaed bronze fountain bubbled in the courtyard that was visible from the dining room. Blazing pink, white, orange, and yellow flowers bloomed in beds and brightly colored pots surrounding the three-foot tall blue-green boy who was forever pouring water out of a pitcher and into a pool. The brick pavers were still damp from plants being watered. PC noticed sprinkler heads poking out from the various flower beds, and she guessed they were probably on a timer.

"Oh!" cried one lady. "Can we go see the fountain? Is that the one that was imported from Italy in 1828?"

"I hadn't really planned…" He glanced out the picture window to the well-groomed courtyard. "Sure. And yes, it was. The original owner, Samuel Freestone, brought it back with him after a trip to Florence."

He opened the French doors, and the group poured into the small courtyard. Almost immediately, noses began to wrinkle.

"Ewww! What is that smell?" one woman asked.

After a quarter of a century as a homicide detective, PC was well-acquainted with that particular odor. She gestured to a prefab toolshed that stood in the far corner. "I think you have a dead raccoon or something in your shed."

Drew's face went white as he also was hit with the aroma of decomposition. He stalked over to the shed and flung open the door. The stench exploded out of the structure, becoming ten times worse. The tour group converged on the French doors at the back of the house to escape the putrescence. PC went to help Drew.

"What do you think?" She craned her neck to look inside without going much closer. "Something crawled in there and died?"

"Gah!" He raised his hand to block his nose with his hand. "Maybe. That is ripe."

Nah. That one's not more than two or three days old. You should try one that's been in a car trunk for a week in the Houston summer. PC stepped up to the shed. It was about seven feet tall, three feet deep, and five feet wide. Everything else was meticulously organized, but there was a large pile of wadded up landscape fabric that covered the entire floor.

PC lifted a corner and discovered a bright white tennis shoe.

Chapter 2

PC DROPPED THE landscape fabric. "Go inside and get the tour group to move on to the Afters. I'll call the police."

Drew's eyes widened. "Shouldn't I call an ambulance?"

The detective shook her head. "It's a bit late for that."

While Drew was inside rounding up the tour, PC texted Tran.

"10-55d at Drew Burlesconi's house." She had to look at the Azalea Trail program to get the address.

"Confirm you are at death scene?"

"Yes."

"My ETA 10 min"

Woody arrived before Tran, and he handed her a roll of crime scene tape. It hurt her to cordon off Drew's yard, but anywhere that had an access point to the courtyard could potentially have trace evidence. Another two officers arrived, and she was relieved to see them with evidence kits—that first episode back in January at the nursing home where they'd come in without gloves, collection bags, or anything had caused her to question their crime scene investigation competence. The Medical Examiner and a morgue assistant arrived about the same time as Tran.

"Hey, Dr. Mack," Tran waved to the ME.

"So, what's the story?" he replied.

"Ask her—she called it in. She's Detective Sergeant PC Donovan. Retired Homicide. PC, this is our ME. His name is Dr. Mackenzie Chapman, but everybody calls him Dr. Mack."

The detective and the ME nodded to each other.

As they made their way to the courtyard, PC explained how they'd come to find a not-so-recently deceased individual in Drew's tool shed.

There didn't seem to be much trace evidence. No blood, no shell casings, no footprints in the flower bed. An officer removed the landscape fabric and wrapped it up as evidence. The body beneath, dressed in a red sweatshirt, navy slacks, and white running shoes, was basically in a fetal position, turned away from the door. After photos were taken and the body rolled over, PC gasped.

"I've seen that guy. Don't know who he is, but he was at the Valentine's brunch and I saw him… in Drew's gallery a couple of weeks ago."

"Then it's interesting that his body should turn up in Drew's tool shed."

PC hadn't heard Woody approach.

"I'm sure the DA will jump right on that." PC couldn't stop a sarcastic smile.

"Usually, if you find the body at someone's house, that someone is responsible," he retorted.

"First rule of investigation: Assume nothing."

"This is kinda weird," Dr. Mack said, raising his voice to drown out the argument. "There aren't any wounds on him, and there's no blood anywhere around him."

"So you think the body was moved here from where he was killed?" Tran jumped in.

"I need to open him up and find out what killed him before I can draw any conclusions. Alright, Phil. Let's load him up and get him to the morgue so I can have a look."

After Dr. Mack and Phil loaded the stranger into a body bag and wheeled him away, Woody turned to Tran. "We need to search the house."

PC peered into the toolshed. The floor was about as clean as could be reasonably expected. A handful or two of mulch here, some stray leaves there. She almost didn't see it. Pushed against the wall in the back corner was a ragged slip of paper. "Hey, what's this?"

Woody came over. "What do you see?"

"Back left corner."

"Gorman!" Woody yelled to an officer who was about to go into the house. "We've got something here."

PC was proud of how carefully he used a tweezer to pick up the object and put it in the evidence bag. It was a corner of good quality paper with the word "Justice" typed on it. *Did the killer think justice had been served?*

She started to head inside, but Woody stepped in front of her.

"Not you."

She wanted to shove him out of the way as he towered over her, but kept her cool. "Your guys just missed a piece of evidence. I think you need all the help you can get at this point."

"One, you're not on the payroll at this time; and two, you're not impartial."

"And you are?" PC instantly regretted saying that. She usually had better control of her emotions. Woody was right—she wasn't impartial, and that galled her to no end. She forced out an apology she really didn't feel. "I'm sorry. That was out of line."

"Yes, it was. Now, the Primrose I knew way back in high school wouldn't be caught dead on an Azalea Trail, so I'm guessing your mama is at the Afters. Why don't you go find her and have some scones?"

PC sucked in a deep breath and let it out slowly. Even after forty years, he could get under her skin faster than a nest of chiggers. She refused to react and give him the pleasure of knowing that he'd gotten to her. She held up her pink-banded wrist and smiled.

"That's a great idea. I think I will go to the Afters and have some afternoon tea while you're here trying to sniff out decomp fluid."

She turned on her heel and strode out the front door, only to see a police cruiser pulling away with Drew, still dressed in his Georgian style clothing, in the back seat. *Calm down. They're only taking him for questioning. I'll get Mama and Justice back home, then go to the station. Who knows? Maybe they will have cut him loose by then.*

Rose had probably done enough walking today, so PC went to the courthouse to pick up the car and drive it to the Afters. She was angry that Drew had been detained, but she knew it was standard procedure. She would have done it herself, if it were her case.

They'd question him. He wouldn't know anything. They'd let him go. Right? If he knew there was a dead body in his toolshed, he wouldn't have opened the door in front of the entire Azalea Trail tour, would he? Of course not.

Unless.

Unless he planned the whole thing as a stunt to make him look innocent. He'd need ice in his veins to pull that off. Like a sociopath.

Have I gotten him completely wrong? She didn't think so. She'd actually interviewed a serial killer once. Every alarm bell in her body had gone off so loudly she could barely hear him talk.

But what did she know about Drew? He owned The Best Little Art Gallery in Texas. Held Saturday afternoon painting workshops with local artists there. He was a retired insurance salesman. Divorced with two adult kids and an ex-wife who looks like a super-model. His grandmother owned an apartment building in New York City. He liked to play darts and drink pale ale. Earned money during his college years sharking pool.

She pulled into a parking slot as close to the entrance of the Afters as she could get. Ordinarily, she'd be disappointed at the prospect of turning down a fancy pastry, but she couldn't eat anything right now. With any luck, Justice and Rose would be done with their food and ready to go.

PC spotted Imogene sitting at a white wrought-iron table under an umbrella.

"Hi. I was looking for Rose and Justice. Do you know where they've wandered off to?"

"Oh sure, darlin'. Your mama's hip was startin' to give her a little grief, so Daisy took them home."

Guilt pricked her, but Daisy was just as much Rose's daughter as she was. Nothing wrong with her sister shouldering some of the load.

"Thank you so much. Have a good afternoon."

"You too, sweetie."

PC went straight to the police station to find Drew. *I wonder if Daisy dropped Justice at her house, or if she's at home with Mama? Justice… no, couldn't be.* She couldn't imagine her mother's friend killing someone and stuffing him in Drew's tool shed. But she'd have to ask.

She pulled up at Possumwood PD, which was, of course, located on Justice Avenue—so was the courthouse. *Could the "Justice" on that slip of paper have been part of an address?* PC liked that idea better than the thought of Rose's friend as a suspect.

An older officer sat at the front desk. PC didn't recognize him, and she wasn't close enough to read his name tag. Tran was talking to him and looked up to see who was coming in the door.

"Hey, PC. You come to look at those cold case files?"

She wasn't sure if he was serious, or being smarmy. He'd never been that way before, so she chose 'serious.'

"Not this time. I was looking for Drew Burlesconi. They brought him in for questioning a little while ago, and I wanted to see if he was still here."

"He's still being interviewed." Tran replied evenly. His voice was carefully controlled and gave away nothing.

PC knew that she would lose if she tried to force him to choose between her and Woody. But she would take any bones he threw her.

She nodded and shrugged, finishing with a hint of a smile. "I understand. I was just wondering if he needed a ride home or anything."

Tran cocked his head. "You know he lives like four blocks from here, right?"

"Have you seen how he's dressed?"

"Good point." He seemed to be considering something. "Let me go check."

"Thanks."

Tran used a card key and disappeared through a grey metal door. She was close enough now to read the silver name tag on the chest of the officer at the front desk. "Stanford"

PC tried to keep her smile somewhat south of insane, but a little north of pleasant, while she racked her brain, searching for any Stanfords she might have known when she was growing up in Possumwood. She came up empty.

Tran returned from his sojourn to the interrogation room and handed her a sheet of notebook paper with a few lines of tidy handwriting on it.

Thanks for checking in. Could use a change of clothes. Key is underneath pot with crown-of-thorns plant. If I'm not home by Monday lunchtime, please call this number and ask for Mason.

The digits were a little spidery, and PC didn't recognize the area code, but she folded the paper and put it in her pocket.

"I'll be back in a little bit."

She drove to Drew's house, wondering if Woody was still there and hoping that he wasn't. Crime scene tape shivered in the breeze and all the interior lights were on. It looked like most of the law enforcement vehicles in Mirabella County were parked outside of Drew's house. PC felt an icy knot form in her stomach.

Have they found something?

Chapter 3

CARS ARE FAST, but radios are faster. Woody met PC at the door. "I heard you were on your way over."

"Are you going to let me in?"

He stepped back so she could come into the parlor. PC looked around at the mayhem that had engulfed Drew's normally tidy front room. She'd always told her investigators to be thorough, but gentle. Somebody was going to have to clean up after their investigation, whether it was a heartbroken loved one or a proven-innocent suspect. Or sometimes a crime scene clean-up service. No point in making more work than necessary for them, either.

It looked like an F5 tornado had swept through. Too fast, too careless. How would they even realize if they'd found anything? But she was already standing on ice that probably wouldn't continue to hold her weight, so she bit back her criticism.

"Your guys find anything?"

Woody crossed his arms over his chest, tucking his fingers into his pits and leaving his blue-gloved thumbs pointing at the ceiling. The right one tapped a few times on his chest.

"No."

Good. PC cleared her throat. "I came to pick up a change of clothes for Drew."

"Okay. After you."

She held up her hands, palms to the ceiling. "You want to drop a hint or two where we're going?"

"You don't know where the bedroom is?" His arms uncrossed.

PC's hands flew to her hips. "First of all, why would I know, and second, why is it any of your business, either way?"

A smirk spread across Woody's face. "Up the stairs, past the sitting room, first door on the left."

The ornately carved mahogany bannisters were long, graceful curves up to the second floor and opened to a sitting room that must have been the height of Georgian fashion. She hoped that the green floral wallpaper was an arsenic-free reproduction. A cabinet of light wood with a black marble top stood against one wall. An uncomfortable-looking settee with clawed feet and a matching armchair on each end faced them, with a low, bow-legged table squatting in front of the antique seating arrangement. Behind the unwelcoming furniture, a museum-sized canvas in a gilt frame depicted two Rubenesque women draped in filmy fabrics that left little to the imagination. They were talking to a recumbent, naked man whose slightly raised arm was at just the right height and angle to conceal his purple eggplant. Two horses with a chariot, and a rainbow, also crowded into the picture.

PC continued down the corridor and opened the first door to her left. The bedroom was oversized, taking up nearly a quarter of the second floor. A floor to ceiling paned window bathed the room in the fading afternoon light. Sky-blue watercolor wallpaper gave her a sense of floating, even though her feet were firmly planted on the intricate parquet floor. The bed, centered opposite the window, was a massive and elaborately carved four-poster canopy bed.

This is like living in a museum. Glad I don't have to dust that thing.

A dark cherry armoire loomed in the corner on the same side as the bed, and a dresser with a large rectangular mirror stood against the wall adjacent to the armoire, a door's width or so away.

The only visible things not antique in the room were a recliner at the edge of the window and the floor lamp beside it. She envisioned Drew sitting there, reading. That made PC smile as she crossed the room to gather some of the clothes that were lying on the Persian rug where the investigators had left them. The detective picked through the mess to find slacks and a polo. She considered socks and underwear, but since there was no bag to put things in, PC stuck with the street clothes.

She stood at the window and gazed down at the courtyard. Each wall had either a door or a gate. The side she was standing above had a door into the living room. The side to her right had a door to the garage. In front of her was a gate to a larger, grassy yard, and to her left was a gate to the alleyway where residents left their garbage cans for pick up and utility companies could access their various boxes and meters. This gate, she noted, was the one closest to the toolshed.

The detective pulled out her notebook and made a little sketch.

"See anything interesting?" Woody had moved to stand behind her, too close, invading her space.

Is he trying to intimidate me? "Is that gate locked?" She pointed to the one on the left.

"I'm not sure. I'll have to ask Sanchez—that was her zone."

"Huh. If it's not, then anybody could have come in from the utility easement. Cameras?"

"No cameras."

"That's a shame."

Woody grunted as she accidentally on purpose elbowed him in the ribs as she turned to leave the room. "Oops."

Downstairs, she found a box of tall kitchen garbage bags on the floor and put the clothes into it. Woody veered off to open the front door. Two men came inside. One was Dr. Mack, and she didn't recognize the other.

"Well?" asked Woody. "You got the autopsy results?"

"I've sent off the toxicology samples, but that may take some time. Be surprised if anything turned up though." Dr. Mack said.

Woody rubbed his jaw. "Why's that?"

"The decedent had a heart defect, probably never even knew it. Poor guy had an aortic aneurysm. It ruptured, and there was nothing that could have been done for him. My best guess of time of death is thirty-six to forty-eight hours. I don't think he was there any earlier than Wednesday night or any later than Friday morning."

PC couldn't help herself. "So, you're saying he died, probably on Thursday, of natural causes?"

"I'm sorry. Who are you?" The stranger interjected.

She plastered on a smile and reached her hand out to him. "Detective Sergeant PC Donovan. I don't believe we've met." *He doesn't have to know I'm retired.*

The man looked from Woody to Dr. Mack, then back to PC before he clasped her hand in an uncomfortable grip. "Detective. Sergeant. Donovan." He nodded his head. "I am the Mirabella District Attorney. Travis Bailey? You might have heard of me?"

No, I haven't. "Oh. Is it usual for the Mirabella DA to personally visit death scenes?"

"It is when the deceased is an IRS special agent. His name was Pete Danvers, by the way."

PC blinked. She was not expecting that. "Really. Possumwood seems like an odd place for someone like that."

"Even small towns are not immune to white-collar crime, Detective." Bailey gave her a greasy smile. "Danvers' supervisor is coming down to claim the body and provide information about his current cases."

"Huh. You'd think they could just email that to you so Woody here could hurry up and close the case." PC ran a hand through her close-cropped hair.

"Well, they have to sanitize it for any confidential information." His eyes narrowed.

"Of course." PC hoisted the bag with Drew's clothes over her shoulder like a Santa sack and locked eyes with Woody. "Shall I go pick up Drew?"

"Sure. Maybe he'll tell you why he stashed the body instead of reporting the death."

"And how do you know Danvers didn't conceal himself before his unfortunate demise?"

Woody ran his tongue over his top teeth. "Then I'd be interested to know why an IRS special agent was surveilling him."

Anger flared up in PC. But not at Woody. Herself. He was right. It was very suspicious that an IRS special agent was found dead, concealed in Drew's courtyard, regardless of how the man died. She was letting her relationship with him interfere with the examination of the evidence.

"Then let's ask him. I'll be back soon."

As she pivoted to close the front door behind her, the trash bag of clothes slipped off her shoulder and snagged on something. The crown of thorns plant. Two-petaled red flowers topped vicious spiked stems that bulged out of the white ceramic pot and over-hung the sides. She freed the bag and continued to her car. *Glad I didn't have to move that monster to get the key.*

Drew was waiting for her in the lobby of the Possumwood PD when she arrived. The frock coat was draped over his arm and the violet vest unbuttoned.

"You okay?" She handed him the slightly worse-for-wear sack.

"Of course. Thank you very much." He took the bag and looked around.

Bourgeois pointed a thumb over his left shoulder. "You can change in that storage closet over there."

When he returned, both to the lobby and the twenty-first century, he patted the trash bag and smiled. "Let's go."

Once they were alone in the car, PC said, "The body in the toolshed. I saw that guy in your gallery on Saturday afternoon, just before Wilma's acrylics class. You had gone over to talk to him as I was going into the classroom. I heard him tell you he was trying to stretch his legs because he was feeling cooped up in his hotel room. Do you have any idea who he was?"

Drew paused while he buckled his seat belt. "I think I know who you're talking about. He came into the gallery a couple of times, but he never bought anything. He seemed really interested in the Patrick Daun painting—he asked me a lot of questions about it."

"Do you recall if there was anyone else that was also there at the same time as him?"

"If there was, I didn't connect the two. Some clients, like Sylvia Marberger, Victoria Deen, and Winnie Hargraves, are redecorating and it seems like they're in the gallery almost every day. Sylvia's husband bought a condo in Houston, and Winnie's updating the City Café décor. I guess Victoria wanted to re-do her space since her husband is out of the picture."

PC shrugged.

A few minutes later, she pulled up in front of Drew's house. The law enforcement vehicles had started to dissipate. She let out a deep breath. "Before we go in, I have to warn you that they did a very thorough search of your house. They took everything out, but they didn't put anything back. Prepare yourself for a mess."

"Thanks for the heads up." He rubbed his temple.

As PC and Drew made their way up the walkway, Woody came out to meet them on the front porch. "Evening, Mr. Burlesconi," he said, ushering them inside.

She noticed Drew's jaw clench at the sight of the disarray. Otherwise, he made no reaction. He just gave a curt nod. "Chief Wilson."

Dr. Mack and DA Bailey sat in the front parlor, chatting, when PC and Drew came in, but stopped and looked expectantly at Woody.

It was obvious to PC that the chief's newfound smile was fake, but she wasn't sure if Drew would see through it. "Mr. Burlesconi, do you have any idea how the body of Pete Danvers came to be in your toolshed?"

"No. I don't know him."

"Is there a reason the IRS might be investigating you?"

PC could see that Woody thought he was poised to spring a trap, but Drew's reaction was genuine puzzlement. "No. I can give you my CPA's number, if you'd like to contact her. How are these things connected?"

Woody gathered himself and tried again. "Mr. Danvers was an IRS special agent."

"Really? Huh." Drew coughed. "Did you find a murder weapon? How did he die?"

Woody clearly did not want to lose what little leverage he had by answering this question.

But Dr. Mack piped up, "It appears to be natural causes. He had a heart defect."

Woody's shoulders sagged.

Travis Bailey stood up. "Even if you didn't kill him, abuse of a corpse is still a felony in Texas. Ten thousand dollar fine and two years in jail. Think on that." He turned to Woody. "I'll be seeing you later, Elwood." He nodded toward PC. "Detective Sergeant Donovan."

PC looked up at the ceiling. Harping on penalties was never going to get someone to confess to a crime. This time, though, she believed the suspect was innocent. But she wasn't one hundred percent sure that she was right—did she have good reason to think he was innocent, or did she just *want* to believe it?

Dr. Mack followed Bailey out the door.

PC studied Drew for a moment. Although he wasn't openly expressing anything, he struck her as being more annoyed than nervous—he stood with his feet apart and arms crossed. She doubted she'd be allowed to read the transcript for his interrogation, so she performed one of her own.

"Drew, have you had anyone at your house this week? Like repairmen, solicitors, anything like that?"

"Is it okay with you, Mr. Burlesconi, if I record this conversation?" Woody held up his phone.

"I already told the officer that questioned me all of this stuff. But if you're trying to cross-check, then no, I didn't have any service people come to the house. But I did host a meeting with Dinah Mae from the historical society, and the other historic homeowners on this year's tour, on Thursday evening."

Woody butted in. "Who was there?"

Another jaw clench from Drew. "I'm sure you can put your hands on one of the Azalea Trail programs. But at the meeting, it was me, of course. Dinah Mae, Joe and Amanda Watkins, Donald Weingarten, Phineas Scott… and Ada Dotson."

PC would have given Woody her program, but she'd lost it.

Hoping that the chief wouldn't jump in again, PC asked, "What time did the meeting start? Did anyone leave early or arrive late?"

"We were supposed to get started at seven. Don was fifteen minutes late. We had just gotten rolling when Phineas stepped outside to take a phone call. By the time we'd basically finished business, the Watkinses got into a fight and left separately—she took the car and he started walking, I don't know, maybe ten minutes later." He rubbed his head. "Oh, and Ada went to the restroom."

"Do you know if any of them were in any financial trouble?" Woody asked.

"No. We were on a committee, not at happy hour. Personal matters weren't discussed."

"Not even the Watkinses?" PC cleared her throat again. *Yay oak pollen season.* "What did they fight about?"

"What *didn't* they fight about?" Drew rolled his eyes and shook his head. "This time it was about whether to bring some knick-knack from the shop to the house for the tour."

"What about Dinah Mae?" PC hoped Woody would continue to refrain from asking questions.

"She sat at the kitchen table with me the whole time. Once the fight broke out, everybody else left around the same time as Joe." Drew coughed and rubbed the bridge of his nose.

That's probably enough to get started. Even if the IRS delivers the name of the person being investigated, there can't be a trial without evidence. Sure would be a lot easier if they'd just emailed the case file.

"Drew, you look tired. I've gotta go feed Mama's animals, but I can come back and help you afterward, if you want."

"Thanks, but it'll be faster if I do it myself."

"Goodnight, then."

"Night."

He walked her and Woody to the door and locked it behind them. Even though Woody's car was down the block from hers on the other side of the street, he escorted her to her vehicle. She was starting to wonder if it was some sort of misguided chivalry until he spoke.

"What time you wanna get started tomorrow?"

"On what?"

Woody spread his hands out. "The investigation? What do you think I'm talking about?"

"I thought I was 1) not on your payroll, and 2) not impartial."

"Yeah. Well, I'm putting you on the payroll."

"What makes you think you can afford me?"

"It could be that the IRS guy crawled into Burlesconi's shed and covered himself up before he died. But it's much more likely that someone put him there either shortly before or shortly after. Maybe nobody killed him. I just want to find out what I can and hand it over to the IRS people—they'll probably want to run the show, since Danvers was one of their guys. I could really use your help, Rosie."

"Rosie. There's a blast from the past. Don't call me that."

Woody looked down at the pavement. "I was just trying to—"

"I know what you were trying to do. Rosie died a long time ago. That night someone shot her father and left him to bleed out in his store. That was the end of her. I'm PC now—I clawed my way out of her ashes. Do. Not. Try. To go there."

Woody turned as if to go to his car, but didn't walk away, just stood there for some moments. PC was getting cold, and she wanted to go home—there was still a lot of work to do yet. Finally, he turned partially around so his profile was to her.

"Last PI, we paid $25 an hour."

Now *he wants to talk about money?* "I could easily get a hundred in the private sector."

"That's not in my budget. Thirty-five."

I probably would have taken thirty-five if you hadn't been such a jerk. "Fifty."

Woody scratched his chin for what seemed like half an hour, but was really not more than a minute. "Fine. Fifty. Be in my office at nine tomorrow."

"I'll be there at ten. I have to take care of the animals first."

Chapter 4

WOODY WENT TO his car, and PC got into hers and started it. The slip of paper with the word "Justice" had been gnawing at the back of her mind like a hungry weasel all afternoon. What did it mean? An abstract ideal? Her mother's friend? Part of an address? What about a business name?

PC made her way to where Business Loop 720 turned into the easternmost part of Justice Avenue and drove west. There were plenty of businesses, but she only noted the ones that had the word "Justice" in their names. As she got closer to downtown, there was *Justice Hardware*, then *Justice Lutheran Church*. She was nearly to City Hall when she found *Do It Justice Cleaners*. Along the roundabout that encircled the municipal building, and catty-corner from the police station, was *True Justice Tattoos*. The City Park sat in between the municipal buildings on the east side and the county buildings on the west side, so she had to drive down Municipal Parkway, turn right on Main, then make another right on County Parkway to get back up to Justice Avenue.

On the south side of the roundabout from the courthouse was *Just Ice Cream*. On the north side was *Justice Bail Bonds*. *Justice Avenue Baptist Church* was another block or two further west. She went all the way to where Justice Avenue dead-ended at Mirabella Creek State Park. There was no more Justice.

She'd only added twenty minutes to her travel time. PC used the hands-free to call Rose. "Hey, Mama. I was thinking of stopping at the Lucky Wok on the way home. You and Rocky want anything?"

"Ooh! Yes, I'd like a General Tso's chicken. Brown rice." Her voice was muffled as she pulled the phone away from her mouth and against her cheek. "Rocky, you want anything from Lucky Wok?"

PC pulled into the parking lot—a narrow strip of concrete between the city park and the municipal roundabout. Businesses had popped up like mushrooms in the downtown gridwork, filling out the lots circling City Hall.

"Alright, honey. Rocky says he wants a shrimp lo mein."

"Got it. Be home soon."

PC set the bag of takeout on the kitchen table. Rocky got plates and silverware and they sorted through their boxes of food.

"I'm sorry I didn't get back to the Afters in time to take you and Justice home."

"It's alright. Daisy was glad to oblige. Now you have to tell me what you found in the toolshed!"

"Tools?" Suggested Rocky.

"Ha ha." Rose shook a fork at him.

"It wasn't a what. It was a who. We found a man, who'd probably been in there a couple of days…"

Rose's eyes got big. "Was it a vagrant? We've started having a few of those hanging around."

Rocky almost dropped the shrimp off his fork.

Had Mama forgotten how recently her own son had been living on the streets? "No. Actually, it was an IRS special agent."

"Get outta town!" A noodle hung like a drowned earthworm from the corner of Rocky's mouth.

Rose smacked her spicy sauce-covered lips, and the smell of sweet chili oil diffused through the kitchen. "God bless him! Aren't they all accountants, though? Why was there a dead bean counter in Drew's shed?"

"Well, regular IRS agents are accountants, mostly, but special agents are just like the ones in the FBI, or the Treasury Department, or the ATF."

"So, who killed him?" Rocky asked, poking through his noodles for another shrimp.

"That's the thing. Nobody. The ME said he died of natural causes—he had heart trouble. But he got in that shed somehow, and I don't think he went in there on his own."

"Do you think… Drew…?" Rose took a sip of her water.

"No. If he knew there was a putrefying body in his shed, would he have led the Azalea Trail ladies out there and opened the door?"

"Probably not." Rose put a battered ball of chicken in her mouth and chewed thoughtfully.

"Woody asked me to consult on the case."

Rocky's fork clattered to the table, and Rose paused mid-chew.

"Aw oo shaw dat's a guh ideah?"

"What?" PC scrunched her face.

Rose swallowed. "Are you sure that's a good idea?"

"Yes, Mama. For one thing, I want to make sure Drew doesn't get railroaded. Woody's ready to lock him up and throw away the key. I'm also a way off social security, and I don't want to spend my whole retirement fund before I get there. It wouldn't hurt to take a paying gig from time to time to shore up my cash flow. Even if it means putting up with Chief Elwood Wilson."

PC's house back in Houston was paid for. She'd been able to save and invest the money she hadn't spent on sending kids to college. Her expenses were low, but not zero, so any supplemental income that found its way to her was welcome—she had to keep Cordite in kibble.

"Well, you used to do a lot more than put up with that man." Rose raised an eyebrow.

"We were in high school. That was a long time ago." PC stabbed a piece of broccoli.

"He's never married."

"Neither have I, but it's not because I've been pining after him." There was someone she missed every day of her life, but it wasn't Woody.

Rose shoveled some rice into the General Tso's sauce. "When you first got here in January, you went out of your way to avoid him. Now you're working with him…"

PC's appetite deserted her, and she closed up her box of food. "Mama, this is not the Hallmark Channel. I am here to help you out while your hip is healing, not reunite with my high school sweetheart. I've got to go feed." She put her leftovers in the fridge and strode outside, Cordite bobbing along in her wake.

Pavarotti and his hens were all accounted for, so she picked up the eggs and locked up the chicken coop. Hazel, the three-legged goat, flapped her lips together, reprimanding PC for being so late to serve dinner.

The two donkeys sang an earsplitting chorus of grunts and squeals, and PC hurried to the feed room. Arthur was a large, nearly black, and very sleek Catalan donkey, while Guinevere was short, beige, and fuzzy. They were something of an odd couple, but Arthur depended on Gwen. He was missing his left eye, and she was his seeing-eye donkey. They bickered from time to time, like an old married couple, but she took care of him. Most of the time. PC had to be careful to always approach Arthur from the right, or else risk startling him and suffering Guinevere's wrath. PC'd already been bitten once and didn't much care to repeat the experience.

After she stuffed the hay racks and topped off the water tank, she sat on the back porch steps and watched them eat. Cordite happily sniffed at bushes, then rolled in the grass. At least, PC hoped it was just grass.

The stars glittered like diamond dust, so many more visible than in the city. She gazed at them for a while, too, wondering if Mike was up there somewhere looking down. She ached to feel his arms around her. Hear his crazy jokes that she had always laughed at, no matter how stupid they were. *Damn that drunk driver.* One tear slid down her cheek, and then another. She pulled up her collar to blot her eyes before they turned red and puffy. All the tears in the world would not bring him back.

Trying to distract herself, she looked for a stick to throw for the dog.

"Cordie! Come!"

As he approached, his beige, wiry terrier hair was slicked almost to his body on one side.

And then she smelled it. "Ugh! Cordite! What have you gotten into?"

She reached for the dog to hose him off, but delighted with his newly acquired eau de rotten egg parfum, he danced away from her. He barked with glee as he raced around the yard—a sulfur-soaked, ricocheting bullet. PC was never going to be able to tackle that little greased piglet, so she let him run himself out. Finally, panting, he plopped down at her feet.

That's when she grabbed him by the collar and carried him to the hose cabinet. He complained about the cold water, but she couldn't take him into the house smeared with reeking green sludge. He would get a nice hot bubble bath indoors. PC was tempted to have one, too.

It was 9:58 the next morning when PC pulled into the Possumwood PD parking lot. She went inside to find Tran waiting for her. He led her through the security door and down a grey hallway to a conference room. Woody sat at the table, an open three-ring binder in front of him. He didn't look up.

"I was thinking we'd start with the Watkinses."

PC shrugged. "Sure. Anything... special about them, other than they fight all the time and left separately from Drew's house on Thursday night?"

"Nothing obvious. They seem to do okay with the antique shop. Although..."

Is this story hour at the library? Spit it out. "Although what?"

"If the gossip is to be believed, Joe is maybe a little over-friendly with some of the ladies around town. Don't see why the IRS would care about that."

"If he's skimming money from the business to pay for a girlfriend, he won't be reporting that on his taxes, now will he?"

"There's that." Woody closed the binder.

PC was unsure if that was a test, or if he genuinely hadn't considered it.

He stood up. "But first, we're going to stop by Danvers' hotel room."

"Hopefully, he will have left his case files there. When is his boss supposed to turn up?"

"Tomorrow morning."

Woody breezed out of the dingy conference room and into the lobby. PC and Tran trailed along behind. The chief paused at the front door.

"Tran, make sure you've got a couple of evidence kits. Donovan, you're with me."

Donovan. That was certainly an improvement over Rosie.

They got into his official Tahoe, and Woody backed out of the parking lot. PC cast a longing gaze at her own car—she felt at a distinct disadvantage having to depend on Woody's good graces.

He cleared his throat. "There was no room key on the body. No car keys, either. But we do know he had a rental."

"The person who stashed the body most likely knows where those things are."

"Agreed."

PC sneezed and had to retrieve a tissue from her bag. *Damn pollen.*

The road slipped by under the tires for perhaps ten minutes. Across the street from the marquee of the truck stop, the timeworn sign for the Silver Dollar Saloon hove into view. It overshadowed the "Best Southern Motel" sign, an aged yellow on orange plastic and metal box near the driveway. The hotel itself had vaguely Mediterranean-style arches that held up the overhang of the second-floor walkway, and it was plastered in terracotta stucco. Unassuming brown asphalt shingles stood in for the tile roof that usually went with that kind of architecture. The landscaping consisted of a bedraggled fan palm that drooped at one corner of the building.

Woody slowed and turned on his blinker, waiting for the traffic, all three cars of it, to pass.

Once they'd parked, PC got out of the SUV and studied the building. Maintenance had obviously been deferred for some time. A crack nearly an inch wide bisected the orange stucco about a foot from the ground and along most of the width of the building from the south wall to the center entryway. "No expenses spared for IRS special agents, I see."

Woody was already on his way to the entrance. Was he ignoring her or just didn't hear her? She didn't press the issue.

The interior of the motel wasn't in any better state than the exterior. Vinyl wallpaper bubbled up along seam lines. Near the vending machine, there was a foot-long gash, and the lower edge curled under, revealing primer and concrete.

The desk clerk had two-day-old stubble and a sour, unwashed smell. He handed Woody a large oval plastic key ring with "Best Southern" printed on it in old west font on a lurid orange background. A single key, room number engraved on the top, dangled from a steel ring. It was probably new in the 1970s. PC couldn't recall the last time she stayed in a hotel with an actual metal key.

"Housekeeping cleaned the room on Friday morning."

"Great," Woody mumbled almost under his breath. "Alright, Fred. Thanks."

A concrete and iron stairway adorned each corner of the building. They chose the one closest to the reservation desk and headed up. Woody leaned over the balcony and waved to Tran, who was just getting out of his squad.

"It's 237."

"Gotcha." Tran popped the trunk.

PC and Woody continued around the corner.

231, 233, 235.

"Gloves?" PC asked. The scene was already compromised, no point in making it worse.

"We'll have to wait for Tran."

They heard the shuddering of the stairs as he jogged up. Moments later, he came into view.

Woody gestured at the door. "You brought gloves?"

Tran slung a black backpack off his shoulder and unzipped it. He pulled out a box of nitrile gloves and held it out to PC. Once they'd all donned the thin blue gauntlets, it was go time.

Woody unlocked the door and used the security latch to prop it open. Some light filtered through the edges of the closed curtains, and PC looked near the door for the light switch. The yellowish, low-wattage bulb in the middle of the ceiling was not much of an improvement.

It was hard to tell if the limp brown shag carpet had been vacuumed lately. The AC was off, and the room smelled stale. PC was grateful it had only been warm and not hot recently.

"I'll take the bathroom," she said, flicking on the light.

A three-inch roach scuttled behind the mirror.

Nice.

The bathroom was tiny. A couple of threadbare towels rested on a rickety metal rack that over-hung the toilet like a rusty pergola. If she were sitting on the throne, she could touch the stained curtain of the half-size shower stall with her left hand and the faux marble vanity with her right without fully extending her arms.

Men's toiletries—a toothbrush and toothpaste, shaving gear, and a box of dental floss—took up most of the small counter. PC looked underneath it, hoping to find an envelope with the agent's case files taped behind the sink. No envelope, but there was another roach. This one flew at her, and she let out a strangled cry as she dodged out of the way.

"You okay?" Woody called from the bedroom.

"Yeah. Fine." She shuddered as she watched the bug land on the ceiling and climb into the exhaust fan vent.

Keeping her eyes peeled for more insect activity, she closed the toilet lid and lifted the cover off the tank. Nothing out of the ordinary in there, either. She put it back and searched under and between the two folded towels on the rack. Empty. There was no obvious plumbing panel.

A joke of a trash can was wedged in between the end of the vanity and the toilet. She picked it up and looked under the liner. Nothing. As she moved to set it down, though, an amber prescription bottle caught her eye. It must have fallen off the counter and gotten pushed against the wall by the miniature waste basket when housekeeping cleaned.

PC picked up the half-empty bottle. It was a prescription for Peter Danvers. Tambocor. She set it on the vanity and used her phone to look up the drug. *Wonder if his supervisor knew?*

PC joined Woody and Tran in the sleeping area. "I found this."

Tran retrieved an evidence bag, and Woody gave it a cursory glance before putting it in the sack.

"Wonder what that's for?"

"Treats irregular heartbeat and atrial fibrillation."

"So. He did have a known heart problem after all." Tran said.

There wasn't much to look at in the shabby hotel room. PC noticed a charger for a laptop laying on the small writing desk, but no computer.

"Could it be in the hotel safe?"

Woody snorted. "That's funny. Hotel safe at the Best Southern."

Tran was checking the nightstand drawers.

The one double bed was encased in a polyester bedspread in lurid colors with a twisting abstract design—all the better to hide stains—and it sagged in the middle.

"We should probably check between the mattresses." She didn't make a move in that direction—both Tran and Woody were closer.

They peeled off the blanket and lifted the mattress. Aside from a large, old bloodstain, there was nothing between it and the box spring.

PC pulled open the drapes, and something glinted in the sudden stream of light.

Chapter 5

"WHAT'S THIS?" PC reached down and picked up a shiny object that was lodged between the baseboard and the leg of the writing desk.

She rolled it in her palm. About the size of a raspberry, but more oblong. The body of it was a dark, glossy red and was encircled by gold filigree set with small stones. Diamonds or cubic zirconia? No telling how long it had been there. Better tag it, just in case.

"What'd you find?" Tran rummaged for an evidence bag.

"Not sure. Looks like a fancy bead." She dropped it into the bag, and Tran sealed it, then filled out the label. Woody gave it a once over before placing it in Tran's backpack.

The chief frowned. "This is a bust." He set the room key down on the desk. "Lock it up when you're done, Tran. Come on, Donovan. Let's go talk to Joe and Amanda."

The Watkinses lived downtown, off Justice Avenue—one block up and about a block over from their shop, *Vintage Glory Antiques*. Woody led the way up the half dozen white brick steps to the front porch. The white house was a gothic revival with steeply pitched roof sections topped with decorative finials, and one weathervane. Green decorative timbers matched the green corrugated roof. Dark green shutters, painted with floral folk-art designs, framed each window. Apple green scrollwork edged the balcony on the second floor that doubled as a portico for the front door, and gave PC the feeling that Hansel and Gretel might be hiding in the bushes, waiting to come out and nibble on the siding.

Amanda Watkins answered the door wearing a subdued floral print dress and light makeup.

"Chief Wilson? To what do we owe the pleasure? We only just got back from church—I'm sorry there's no coffee. I can put some on…"

"No thanks. We're good. Can we come in?"

"Of course! Where are my manners?"

By this time, Joe had come to see who was at the door. "What's going on?"

"Well, you've probably heard about the unfortunate incident on the Azalea Trail?" Woody asked.

Amanda breathed in sharply. "I heard about that. I was at Karla's Kurls in the afternoon, and the girl who does my highlights, Daisy, told us all about it."

Lack of facts has never stopped the Daisy Report. PC pulled a tiny Moleskine out of her back pocket to take notes.

Joe shifted his weight. "What's that got to do with us?"

PC stepped forward. "Nothing. Not directly, anyway. The Medical Examiner thinks the victim, Mr. Danvers, died on Thursday. And you attended a Historical Society meeting at Mr. Burlesconi's house on Thursday evening. Would you tell us about that meeting?"

Joe yawned. "We got there. Talked about the Azalea Trail. Amanda left early. I don't know what else there is to say."

"Well," Amanda added, "Drew really knows how to host a meeting. He had a fruit plate, a cheese and cracker plate, and some fancy iced tea with bergamot and lavender. Which was really helpful, since Don was so late."

PC tried to dig a little deeper. "Did you notice anything strange or unusual at that time?"

Joe's eyes narrowed. "Like what?"

"Well," PC jumped in before Woody could ask any questions. "Strangers hanging around anywhere nearby? Any abnormal items in the house? Stuff like that."

"Ha!" Joe plopped down on the sofa. "Most of the items in Drew's house *are* abnormal."

Amanda rolled her eyes to the ceiling and softly shook her head. "At least *he's* interesting." She didn't look at her husband, but focused on the space just past PC's left ear. "The only thing I saw out of the ordinary was on the way home—Victoria Deen's BMW parked on Main Street with the hood up and flashers on, over by the Sweet July store."

"Did you know somebody tried starting a rumor that she's a vampire? During the spring and summer, she only comes out at night." Amanda gave a harsh laugh. "Bees. She's terrified of bees. Of all things." She shook her head. "Anyway. I wasn't worried about her—Tim Kowalski was there helping her out. There's bound to be a hardware joke in there, somewhere."

Woody glanced at PC. "He owns the hardware store."

Justice Hardware? "So they know each other, then." PC said.

"Oh, I'm sure they *know* each other. He usually goes on his morning runs in Spandex tights and I will say, his toolbox runneth over. I don't blame her one bit. I'm sure she's needed comfort in her time of sorrow. Everyone needs to have a handyman in from time to time."

"Amanda! That's enough. They didn't come here to listen to you gossip." Joe snapped.

Huh. I was sure Victoria was one of those three girls that took auto shop back in high school. Maybe I'm misremembering. It's been forty years. Or, she just wanted plausible deniability for her hookup with Tim. But carry on, Amanda. I'm open to whatever gossip you want to share.

The tiniest smirk slid across Amanda's face. "Well, I was home by 8:30, and you could probably walk to where I saw Victoria from here in five minutes. Of course, I don't know if they were still there when my husband passed by. I had a glass of wine and watched TV for over an hour before I fell asleep. Alone."

It took a couple of seconds for Joe to realize his wife had just thrown him under the bus and shifted it into Drive.

"The rest of us, everybody but Drew, went to the Biersal for a drink."

PC made a note to confirm this with the other historical home-owners. Of course, Drew was back to having no alibi, if it was true.

She snapped the book closed. "They sure get creative over there at the Biersal. Have you tried that persimmon ale?"

Joe crossed his ankles and leaned back on the couch. "I have *not* been brave enough to try that one. I stick with either the stout or the IPA."

"Those can go down easy." PC nodded.

Woody opened his mouth, but she shot him a look, and he closed it again.

"Still, it was probably an enjoyable walk from the Biersal back to your house." She tapped the notebook absently.

"Are you kidding me? I didn't walk. Too late—after midnight. I got a ride home." His eyes widened, and he swallowed. "Well, I mean." His head jerked toward the front door, then he gestured over his shoulder. "Phineas Scott's just across the alley."

PC smiled, trying to calm him. "Very sensible, getting a lift. Nothing good happens after midnight, right?"

Of course, he never actually said he rode with Scott, just that his house was nearby. There was clearly something he didn't want his wife to know, and he certainly would not tell the police in front of her. Which is why witnesses are usually separated, but technically it was Woody's case, and it seemed he was only going through the motions, anyway. She sighed inwardly.

Woody coughed. "Joe, Amanda." He nodded at each of them. "Thanks for your time. If you think of anything else, no matter how small, y'all just pick up the phone, alright?"

Amanda opened the door for them. "Y'all have a *nice* afternoon."

The way she said "nice"—with an upward curl of her eyebrow— made PC cringe. What, exactly, did she mean by that?

The Tahoe chirped as Woody clicked the remote.

As soon as the doors were closed, he asked, "What did you think, Donovan?"

"I think we still have Drew without an alibi for the evening, Amanda claiming to be home alone for at least three and a half hours with no one to confirm that, and Joe lying about his ride home. And what about the hardware guy? Is there any chance that the Justice on the note could refer to Justice Hardware?"

Woody pulled out of the parking spot. "There's always a chance…"

Maybe it was the way he trailed off, or perhaps it was the flex and release of his jaw muscle, but PC wasn't entirely sure he was referring to Toolbox Tim.

"Where to next, Chief?"

"I was thinking Don Weingarten's. He's just the other side of the church from here."

The parking lot of Justice Avenue Baptist Church had mostly emptied. A half dozen cars rested in the shade of a thick live oak tree. This was no old country church—its founder, Reverend Joshua Deen, had it custom-built to summon the faithful to come from miles around to worship.

There was something about the way the roof curved up to a point that reminded PC of a ship. A sleek metal cross crowned the ridge of almost white shingles. Below the grey steel, an abstract stained glass rendering of what might have been Jesus on or near a cross, stretched across the entire front of the building. On the red brick courtyard below that, water poured out of the wound in the side of a ten-foot bronze Jesus into a fountain below.

Sometimes the line between tacky and creative can be a bit smudged.

Woody parked at the palatial Victorian house next door to the church, and PC remembered it being the very first one on the Azalea Trail. Zachariah Phineas Prescott Justice, the impresario who'd founded Possumwood, had named it *Fairhaven*. She wondered if the Weingartens ever called it that. PC and Woody went up the stairs to the front door and knocked.

There was no answer.

After about three minutes, Woody said, "We'll come back later. Let's try Ada Dotson's. She owns the downtown liquor store—Dot's. It's catty-corner from the Biersal."

Woody took the courthouse loop to get back to Main Street, then turned onto South Cumberland. Ada's house, *Fallbrook Cottage*, and the fourth on the Azalea Trail, was across the street and about half a block from Drew's.

This house had clearly been expanded after it had been built. It was much more than a cottage at two stories, not counting the attic rooms and the partial basement. Dove grey clapboard siding covered the house, and lacey scrollwork dripped from the eaves of the wrap-around veranda. The glassed-in belvedere reminded PC more of a church bell tower than something that should be on a private home.

The woman who answered the door was probably in her late sixties. PC had only seen her in her Victorian costume, and the modern clothes were jarring. Ada Dotson took a puff on a nearly black cigar before opening the screen door.

"Afternoon, Chief." She squinted at PC. "You look familiar."

"I was on the Azalea Trail yesterday."

"Ah. Why are you two standing out there? Come inside, already."

The biggest fluffy marmalade cat PC had ever seen stared down at them from atop an imposing armoire.

Ada followed PC's eyes. "That's Hennessey."

"Is he part mountain lion?"

"Maine Coon." She turned to Woody. "I heard about that fella you found at Drew's house. I reckon that's why you're here." She moved across the room to where a smoke filtration machine whirred softly on the table. "Can't let the smoke damage the antiques. Historical register and all that."

Woody gave her a *that's-very-reasonable* nod. "Yes, ma'am. You were at Mr. Burlesconi's house on Thursday, for the Azalea Trail tour meeting. Would you tell us about that?"

"Not much to tell. Don was late, as usual. Joe and Amanda got into a screaming fight, as usual, and she left about fifteen minutes before everybody else."

PC picked up the thread. "We were wondering if you recall seeing anything or anybody out of the ordinary, on your way to the meeting, on the way home, or even at Drew's house."

Ada rolled her cigar back and forth between her fingers, the little machine rapidly sucking up the smoke.

"Not really. I noticed there was a card from the tattoo shop on Drew's bathroom vanity." She shrugged. "Seemed out of character, but lots of people have tats, some you'd never guess."

"Which tattoo parlor was it?" PC asked sweetly.

Ada's eyebrows raised. "The only one there is in Possumwood."

True Justice Tattoos. "Oh. Thanks." PC sighed and pretended to be summoning up the courage to ask a question. "Okay, I know this is a little out of left field, but I think it falls under your area of expertise. What do you think of the persimmon ale at the Biersal?"

"You drove out to ask me what I think of persimmon ale?"

"No! Of course not. I'm trying to get up my nerve to try it. And you're an expert. I mean, did you happen to notice if lots of people were drinking it on Thursday night when you went to the Biersal?"

"How would I know? Why would you think I was there?"

PC feigned surprise. "Oh… didn't everyone go out for a drink after the meeting?"

"I wouldn't be caught dead at the Biersal with those idiots. Besides, I had to finish up some online orders—I had a ten PM deadline."

Woody reached for the screen door handle. "Thank you, Ada. You call 'round to the station if you think of anything else, okay?"

"Sure."

Ada stood on her porch and watched them, puffing smoke rings into the clear afternoon sky.

PC slammed the Tahoe door. "What else is Joe Watkins lying about?"

Chapter 6

"WHY ARE YOU so sure Joe is lying?" Woody pulled away from the curb.

"He refused to say who he got a ride with, then he said that everybody except Drew went to the Biersal, but Ada didn't go."

"He said he rode home with the mayor, and maybe Ada never goes to there, so he didn't think to include her in 'everybody.'"

"No, Watkins *didn't* say he rode with the mayor. He said the mayor's house was across the alley. That's not the same thing. And if he specifically excluded Drew from going to the Biersal, it seems reasonable he would also exclude Ada. But you might be right. Not much daylight between evasive and lying, though."

Woody pulled onto Main. "I thought we'd try Don Weingarten again."

"Back to the palace, huh?"

"Yeah. I guess you got the tour yesterday." Woody waited for a car to merge into the roundabout.

"Please. How many school field trips did we have there? The empresario's mansion—and he may as well have been the governor—for his little group of what was it? Two hundred settlers?"

Woody snorted. "Where else but the governor's mansion would you expect a retired hedge fund manager to live?"

He stopped the Tahoe in front of the Weingartens' palace. Pale limestone bricks shown in the afternoon sun, and the frilly black wrought iron railings that bordered the second and third-floor balconies, as well as the veranda, were a stark contrast. Slate fish-scale tiles topped the fairy-tale castle tower, drawing the eye upward to leering gargoyles along the eave. A white-framed greenhouse, its bronze roof structure a grey-green patina, peeked out from behind the main building.

PC opened her door. "Let's see if His Eminence is home."

She paused between the pair of marble lions, softened by time, that guarded the staircase to the entryway. Their cavernous maws would make excellent places to conceal security cameras. But if there were any in their open mouths, they were very well hidden.

Sofia Weingarten answered the door. "Chief Wilson?"

"Afternoon, Ms. Weingarten. Can we come in?"

"Of course." She smiled, then paled. "Is there anything wrong at the bank?" Apprehension edged her voice.

"No. No, ma'am. The bank is fine. Is your husband home?"

Don Weingarten ambled into the foyer, a drink in his hand. The glass held a clear liquid on ice, with a wedge of lemon clinging to the rim.

Water or vodka?

"Afternoon, Chief." He gave PC an up and down scan. "Who's your friend?"

"This is Detective Sergeant Donovan. She's just recently come back home from Houston."

Until Mama's hip heals. PC gritted her teeth and smiled. "Afternoon."

Sofia shifted, and PC caught a waft of her perfume. *Floral. Expensive.*

Don gestured with his free hand. "What can we do for Possumwood's finest today?" His smile was distinctly insincere.

Woody started. "There was an incident—"

"What kind of incident?" Sofia broke in.

PC stepped in. "Unfortunately, a body was discovered Saturday during the Azalea Trail. Dr. Chapman thinks he died on Thursday."

"I heard about that." Don nodded. "In Burlesconi's shed, right?"

"Yes." PC got out her notebook.

Sofia gasped. "A murder?"

"No, ma'am." Woody's voice was soothing. "He died of natural causes."

PC stepped in to get the conversation back on track. "Since you were at Mr. Burlesconi's house on Thursday evening, Mr. Weingarten, would you tell us about that meeting?"

Don took a sip of his drink. "I was a little late because Sofia's Mercedes wouldn't start, so I had to drop her off at Truffles! for her bank board of directors dinner." He waved his drink-free hand dismissively. "There are only so many historic homes in Possumwood, so we've all done this Azalea Trail thing at least once. Nothing new at the meeting. Joe and Amanda got into a spat and she left early. I went to Truffles! and sat in the bar until Sofia's meeting finished. Then we got home," he looked at his wife, "nine-thirty? Ten?"

"That sounds about right."

"So you chose to go to Truffles! instead of the Biersal with the others from the meeting?" PC probed.

"Nobody said anything to me about that. Not my kind of place, though. I'll get their bottled beer at Dot's but I wouldn't say I'm a regular in the brew pub—their stout is good, but the other stuff is too gimmicky. I mean, have you seen that persimmon ale they've been pushing?" He grimaced and stuck out his tongue.

Interesting. Did anybody *actually go to the Biersal that night?* "During the afternoon or evening, did you notice any strangers, or anything unusual or out of place?"

Don shook his head. "No. I don't remember anything."

Sofia rubbed her shoulder and chewed her lip. "It's probably nothing. But now that you mention it, on the way home, I saw a car parked at Vintage Glory. I probably wouldn't even have remembered, except it had Alabama plates."

"What kind of car?" Woody asked.

"Hmmm. I'm not really sure. It was little, but it had four doors. Either white or silver—it was dark when we drove by."

Could that be Danvers' rental car, parked at the Watkins' store? "That's helpful. Thank you. Did you see anyone inside, or standing near it?"

"Not that I noticed, no."

Woody reached for the door. "The Possumwood PD appreciates your help. If y'all remember anything else, just call down to the station."

The silent lions watched PC and Woody get into the Tahoe. If they knew anything about Pete Danvers, they weren't telling.

Woody started the truck. "What do you think about the car parked at the antique shop?"

"Sounds like a rental. I can't imagine there's a big enough draw in Possumwood to entice someone all the way from Alabama."

He pulled away from the curb. "Unless they were just passing through."

"Possumwood isn't exactly on the way to anywhere. Do we know what kind of car Danvers had, and where he got it? Rental car companies these days can track their vehicles—has it been reported to them?"

"I'm not sure if the IRS has done that or not."

PC ran her tongue over her teeth. "Okay, if that was his rental, then somebody took it somewhere. Was it the person who hid the body, or a garden variety auto thief?"

"We don't have too many kids boosting cars around here. Picks up in the summer..."

"What about cameras?" *Surely at least some shops downtown had them.*

"Truffles! might have one. I think the Afters has 'em in their parking lot. Of course, there are cameras at the city and county buildings, but those aren't close enough to Vintage Glory."

"It's been a few days, so anything that was there on Thursday is probably gone now, but I think we should stop by Vintage Glory and look at their parking area."

Woody shrugged. "It's on the way to Mayor Scott's."

PC knew that there was little likelihood of finding anything, but he didn't have to make it so obvious that he was just humoring her.

He parked at Drew's gallery, the next-door neighbor to Vintage Glory.

"I'll go check for cameras," he said before opening his door.

At least it isn't hot.

The general parking for downtown was comprised of slanted spaces in front of each building, so the customer parking area for each business was small. PC scanned the debris in the gutter. A crushed styro cup. A candy wrapper. Two bottle caps. A few pieces of a broken bottle.

Hello! What's that?

Chapter 7

A BRIGHT RED rectangle of opaque plastic, less than an inch wide with two flat metal prongs sticking out like blunted fangs, lay next to one of the pieces of broken glass. The number ten was printed in yellow along the spine. It looked like an electrical plug, only much flatter and without the cord.

Huh. Probably just another piece of random garbage, like the rest of it.

She searched the Tahoe and found a single evidence bag. There were no gloves, but she had a dog poop sack in her pocket. She stuck her hand inside it and very carefully collected the debris from the gutter.

PC had just sealed the evidence bag when Woody left the Truffles! parking lot and jogged across the street.

"They do have a camera, but it faces the other way. Find anything?"

"Probably just trash, but I bagged it anyway."

A smug smile gripped the corners of his mouth. He got into the truck and started the ignition.

"Let's go see the mayor."

Phineas Scott's house had been right in the middle of the tour. Back in 1830, a disgraced French diplomat—Francois de Lamartine—had fled a romantic scandal and settled in Possumwood, but hadn't left the sophistication of Paris behind with his custom-designed home. Local legend had it he'd hidden a cache of his mistress' jewels somewhere in the house, but nothing has ever been found.

The first floor sported a wraparound veranda, the second, crisp white clapboard, and the third crowned the house with a mansard roof in dark slate grey, punctuated with dormers and fringed with a wrought iron widow's walk. A central tower highlighted the entrance, with a circular drive curving under a carriage portico on the ground floor, and balustraded balconies on the other two. PC remembered this house still had the original Italian marble black and white chessboard floor. It was also the house with the orange and red azaleas.

She felt like they were being watched as they got out of the car and walked to the opulent front door. Although it was pleasant in the sun, she found it a bit too cool for comfort in the shade of the grand entryway's overhang, and pulled her arms against her body.

Woody rang the doorbell, and a dog started barking. It trotted into the entry way and PC caught glimpses of it through the beveled glass. The pup was dark and medium-sized, but there was something odd about it.

A man came into view behind the glass.

"Anubis. Sit!"

The dog quieted and sat, and the man opened the door.

Woody nodded. "Afternoon, Phineas."

The mayor was wearing a red Hawaiian shirt and cargo shorts, and PC noted a pair of Birkenstocks by the door. The only things he was missing were a Panama hat and an umbrella drink.

"Hey, Chief!" Phineas pivoted and reached for PC's hand. "Do we know each other? I feel like we've met."

I'm not registered to vote in Mirabella County, Slick. "Azalea Trail, yesterday."

"Of course! I remember now. You were with Rose Donovan—you must be her daughter."

"Yes. I'm Detective Sergeant Donovan."

The mayor's eyes widened, and he let go of her hand.

"But you can call me PC."

Her eyes strayed to the dog which hadn't moved since it sat down on the marble floor. It was completely black, with large, bat-like ears. And no hair. Save for a few tufts on top of its head, it was bald. But the eyes. They were gold and wolf-like, watching suspiciously above muscular jaws.

Woody turned to her, "I should have warned you, he's got a pet Chupacabra."

Phineas leaned over and patted the dog on the head, "Nubie is a Xoloitzcuintle, but Mexican Hairless is easier to pronounce. Did you want to come inside, or are you happy to stand on the porch?"

PC followed Woody into the house.

"So. What brings you two out to my humble abode this afternoon?"

Woody cleared his throat. "It's about that IRS agent. Dr. Mack said he most likely died on Thursday, so we were having a chat with everybody that was at the meeting at Drew's house Thursday night."

"What do you want to know?"

"Could you tell us about the meeting?" PC asked as she took out her notebook.

"Well… Dinah Mae gave us a refresher on Azalea Trail protocol. I had to step outside to take a phone call from Norm at the Drainage District, but apparently, I didn't miss anything. Joe and Amanda seemed especially hostile, and she left early. I came home and walked Anubis."

PC looked up. "You came straight home from the meeting?"

"Well, yeah. Why wouldn't I?"

"It was our understanding," Woody purred, "that some of the homeowners went to the Biersal afterward."

"Nobody said anything about that to me. I wouldn't have gone anyway—like I said, I had to walk Nubie. He gets separation anxiety if he's home alone for too long."

He gave the dog an affectionate scratch on the head. Anubis continued to glare disapprovingly at PC and Woody.

"Tell us about the trip home." Woody cleared his throat.

"Ada and I both walked. She's just one house over and across the street from Drew. I'm less than ten minutes away, and I prefer to walk whenever I can. Anyway, when we got to Ada's house, there was a guy standing on the other side of the street in the Little Gallery's employee parking area talking on his phone. He didn't look dangerous—he even waved at us. But I made sure Ada was safe inside before I continued. Anybody breaking into her house is taking their life in their own hands, though."

PC scribbled in the Moleskine. "Do you think you'd recognize this man if you saw him again?"

Phineas shook his head slowly. "I doubt it. It was pretty dark, and the security light at the back of the gallery isn't very bright. I think he was wearing a red shirt, but it was hard to tell, dark pants and really bright white tennies, like they were fresh out of the box. More than that, I can't say with any certainty."

Danvers was wearing a red sweatshirt, dark pants, and white athletic shoes.

PC resisted the urge to look over at Woody.

"Around what time was this?" PC's pencil hovered above the paper.

"We left Drew's around 8:45 and I was home before 9:00."

PC coughed. "Did you go straight out to walk your dog? Where did you take him?"

"Yes. I came in, grabbed the leash, and off we went. Took one of our usual routes, down the utility easement along the back of the houses to Morgan Road, then we went down that to Main and back home. You know, as soon as we got outside, I did notice a car pulling into the drive at the Watkinses. Didn't think much of it, just figured somebody was dropping Joe off."

"Did you see the car?" Woody asked.

"No, just the glare from the headlights coming through the back fence. I didn't really pay much attention. I was busy… scooping. That's one of my pet peeves, you know—people who don't pick up after their dogs. I'm happy to lead by example." He scowled. "I only really remember it because the glare was making it harder to find all the nuggets."

The corner of Woody's mouth twitched. "Do you recall anything else?"

"No. Not really."

"If you think of anything, just give me a call, or drop by my office."

"You've been a big help, Mr. Scott," PC added. Her gaze dropped to the dog. His yellow eyes fixed on hers. And the message was obvious: *Get out of my house.* She wasn't one to argue.

Woody started the engine. "I think we're down to the last witness—Dinah Mae Brown. She actually lives onsite at the Quenton Plantation—she manages the place."

"I wonder if she knows where Joe Watkins was after the meeting."

Chapter 8

PC WATCHED THE scenery fly by as Woody drove. On one side of the road, things looked much the same as she remembered them. The other side was unrecognizable. The house, barn, and pasture where her best friend had lived and kept her horses and sheep had been replaced by a concrete pad and an ugly self-storage complex. A hundred yards further down, an immense warehouse smothered the prairie where they used to pick dewberries. Change is the only constant. She knew that. But sometimes change was flat out ugly.

Beyond that, a gas station with a convenience store and restaurant was nearing the end of construction. When that new tollway came through next year, they were hunkered down in prime locations. She wondered if the Quenton Plantation Historical Park would reap a bounty of fresh visitors from the city.

A glance at the Tahoe's clock told her they were only about halfway through the twenty-minute trip.

Woody's voice startled her. "You figured it out yet?"

It took her a second to bounce back. "Colonel Mustard in the library with the lead pipe."

He didn't reply.

She tried again. "So far, nobody has an alibi that can be corroborated. Unless you can get Anubis to talk. And what about Amanda Watkins? Either she didn't get home when she said she did, or she had a visitor. Could it have been Danvers?"

"If the car with the Alabama plates that Sofia Weingarten saw was his, he couldn't have stayed long. She saw the car parked between 9:30 and 10 at the store."

"What if he picked Amanda up, and they drove back to the shop?" PC mused.

"I doubt Amanda Watkins weighs ninety pounds soaking wet. I have a hard time believing she could wrestle someone twice her size in dead weight into Burlesconi's shed. You think she fireman-carried him down Main Street and around the corner?"

"No. I don't think she carried anybody. But if someone were to walk across the employee parking of the antique shop and take the utility easement along the back of the houses instead of the sidewalk, it's probably not fifty yards."

"I guess that makes sense, since there was a man behind the art gallery when Ada and the mayor walked home."

Gravel crunched as Woody turned off the highway onto the park road. PC had always liked the stately avenue of pecan trees, whose shaggy branches reached out to caress each other across the white caliche drive.

"I suppose," she said, "Assuming that was him, the question is who was he talking to on the phone? Was he setting up a meeting? Did his mother call him at just the wrong time? Did he have car trouble? Was it towed?"

"I assume the IRS can get their hands on his phone records pretty quickly. And once they get here tomorrow, I'm sure they're gonna want to take over, since Danvers is their guy. I figured folks would be more apt to talk to me than the tax people. Looks like he died of natural causes, and whoever he was surveilling, well, that's their business. Right now, there's no evidence he didn't crawl into Gillespie's shed on his own." Woody shrugged. "Maybe somebody stole his car, but it could have been towed. We're still calling lots within a fifty-mile radius."

PC clenched her jaw shut. She couldn't imagine walking away from an investigation, even if it wasn't a murder. It was still a suspicious death. And her friend had been implicated.

"I thought your DA was eager to charge somebody with abuse of a corpse."

"Travis?" Woody snorted. "You know how lawyers are. I doubt he'd want to waste his budget on prosecuting a case like that. Especially if the Feds are looking to prosecute for something bigger."

I still need to know for sure that Drew wasn't involved.

Woody turned into the lot and pulled into a space.

These trees are a lot bigger than I remember. Gnarled, squat live oak trees, dripping with wiry Spanish moss, shaded the parking area. PC was glad of that shade, because as the sun had trekked past noon in the cloudless sky, the day had gotten uncomfortably warm.

The walkway to the ticket office, a small cinderblock building off to the side of the plantation house, was paved, and an ADA friendly ramp sloping up the six steps to the front porch of the mansion was new, at least since the last time she'd visited. And that was on a school field trip. The ticket office was inside the house back then. The plantation house had seemed so mind-bogglingly enormous then. Now it was merely big.

A teenager, dressed in 1830s settler garb, manned the booth. She quickly stowed her phone as they approached.

"Afternoon," Woody said. "Is Miz Brown here? We'd like to have a word."

Her hands trembled a little as she picked up the desk phone and pushed the number three. "Yes, ma'am. There's somebody here from the po-lice to see you... okay."

"She'll be right up."

A few minutes later, a golf cart rolled up from the livestock area. Dinah Mae Brown, dressed in jeans and a plaid flannel shirt, sleeves rolled up, parked and stepped out of the cart. A few strands of hay dangled from her loosely pulled-back hair.

"Well, my, my. Chief Wilson, to what do we owe the honor?" Her long eyelashes fluttered.

She's been re-enacting so long she can't get out of character.

"Can we speak in your office?" Perspiration beaded on Woody's forehead and he shifted his weight.

He must be burning up with that ballistic vest on. Bet he's desperate for the AC. She had a moment of feeling under-dressed without the lightweight vest she had always worn out in the field. It was rare, but detectives sometimes got shot at, and a stylish blazer is only a couple of millimeters better than nothing at stopping a bullet.

Dinah Mae tapped on the ticket window. "Cassandra, can you buzz us in?"

They followed Dinah Mae around the corner to a secure entryway. The lock clicked, and cool air rushed out as Dinah Mae pushed the door open.

"My office is the first door on your right. I need to avail myself of the facilities."

They made their way to Dinah Mae's cramped office and surveyed the seating arrangements. Woody sat in the chair closest to the wall, but had to turn sideways because there wasn't enough room for his long legs. PC pulled her own seat out past the wooden desk. Otherwise, she would be practically sitting in his lap. Cassandra came in and set three bottles of cold water on the desk, then hurried back to her post.

Woody grabbed one and drank half of it down in one gulp.

Files and loose papers littered Dinah Mae's under-sized desk. A marked-up flyer for the upcoming Settlers' Day Festival in June lay under a green and brass banker's lamp.

The Quenton Plantation manager entered the office, wiping her hands on her thighs. She'd plucked the hay out of her hair and applied lipstick. PC guessed she was mid to late thirties, and she was a handsome woman. Dinah Mae sat primly in her office chair, legs together at the knees, and feet tucked behind and to one side, even though she wasn't wearing a skirt.

"Now, how may I help y'all this afternoon?"

She said *you all*, but she only looked at Woody.

He leaned forward in his chair. "Well, I don't have to tell you what happened on the Azalea Trail yesterday."

If she had been wearing pearls, she surely would have clutched them.

"I have never been so humiliated in all my born days. I just don't know if we'll be able to hold the Azalea Trail next week, or even the rest of the month. It *is* the Historical Society's biggest fund-raiser, you know. If people stay away, who's going to bid on the silent auction items? And most of the shops in town have Azalea Trail specials, where they donate sales to the Society. Who's going to shop for those? We may have to add bake sales to make up the difference."

It wasn't such a great experience for Pete Danvers, either.

"I understand. Finding a deceased person is shocking." Woody nodded ever so slightly. "But what we really wanted to ask you about was the meeting on Thursday night at Mr. Burlesconi's house. Would you mind telling us about that?"

"The meeting? Well…" Dinah Mae pursed her lips "We were late getting started because Don Weingarten didn't arrive until almost 7:15. The quality of the Azalea Trail experience is very important, and it is vital that everybody is very, *very* familiar with the protocols before the event. I wish the mayor had understood that, instead of interrupting the meeting to take a phone call. At least when Ada's phone kept ringing, she left it on silent. Although, I will say, it was quite distracting every time it vibrated on the table. As soon as Mayor Scott stepped outside, she said she needed the ladies' room. And thank goodness she took her buzzing phone with her." A finely plucked eyebrow arched up Dinah Mae's forehead. "All I asked for was an hour. One hour, to make sure the Azalea Trail remains a top-quality event."

Everyone else remembers Joe and Amanda getting into a fight and her leaving early. Did Dinah Mae forget, or is she deliberately not mentioning it? PC let Woody do all the talking, since he was the focus of Ms. Brown's attention. She retrieved one of the water bottles on the desk and took a sip.

The chief smiled at the director. "Dinah Mae, you are being so helpful."

She batted her eyelashes at him.

"Do you remember seeing any strangers, somebody or something out of place on Thursday?"

"No. Do you think I drove around town sightseeing after the meeting?"

Defensive. She's covering something up.

"Of course not." Woody tried soothing her. "Since the… unfortunate event happened at Mr. Burlesconi's, and the meeting was held there, we just thought that one of you good folks might have seen something. And there was a mention of drinks at the Biersal."

Dinah Mae's eyes flashed, and her lips pursed. "The Biersal. W-I did not go to the Biersal."

Was she going to say, "We did not go to the Biersal?"

"Did you go anywhere after the meeting?"

"Home. I had skipped lunch, and I was famished." A blush rose on her cheeks.

PC took another sip of water. *Oh, Dinah Mae. What are you not telling us? Amanda Watkins had raved about the food Drew had out for the meeting.*

Woody shifted in his chair and untangled his legs. "Thank you so much, Dinah Mae. We'll give you a call if we have any more questions."

The three of them rose, and Dinah Mae escorted PC and Woody to the exit.

As soon as they were out of earshot of the ticket window, PC said, "Joe Watkins was being evasive, and Miss Brown was *also* being evasive. Suppose those two things are related?"

Woody glanced over his shoulder, as if he wanted to make sure no one was listening in. "Unless they were moving Pete Danvers' body, it's really none of my concern."

"Neither one of them told us the whole truth, so maybe they were."

"That's certainly a possibility."

The silence between them was uncomfortable, and PC focused her attention on the twisting branches of the live oaks. The three-minute walk felt like three hundred minutes.

The Tahoe chirped as they approached, then they got inside. As soon as her seatbelt was buckled, PC took another sip of water. Woody gulped the rest of his down and punched a button on the steering wheel.

"Call Tran."

Woody surprised PC with his brusque command. On principle, she resisted reaching for her device.

The screen on the center console changed to the icon of a phone handset.

"Calling Hiro Tran," the vehicle's computerized voice replied.

The officer answered.

"We're coming in. Could you get pizza for us and everybody at the station from Zeno's?"

"Will do. Anything else?"

"That's it. Thanks." He poked the "end" button on the screen and backed out of the parking space. "Alright. I think we're done gallivanting. When we get back to the station, this is what I need you to do, Donovan. Type up the reports of the witnesses we interviewed today. I'll sign off on it, then when you get me an invoice, I'll get Henrietta to cut you a check."

"So you're not planning on any further investigation?"

"Nope. I'm handing it all off to the IRS. He was their guy, I think they're going to want to handle it. They had Danvers surveilling somebody, and they aren't going to share that with us. But I am curious. What's your theory?"

The plastic bottle crackled in PC's hands. "My theory? I think that Pete Danvers was alive at 8:45, when the meeting broke up, and he was possibly arranging to meet someone. Was he the one blowing up

Ada's phone? Nobody has a rock-solid alibi, and at least three people are hiding something—both Watkinses and Dinah Mae. But without looking deeper into the witnesses and knowing who the IRS was investigating, I can't do anything more than guess."

The Tahoe bumped along on the caliche.

"And what is your guess?"

PC sighed. *Why is he asking me this?* "I don't really like to speculate without evidence."

"Fair enough."

The pizza had been better than PC expected, and she probably shouldn't have eaten that last slice—she was feeling drowsy after such a heavy meal. The detective was doing a basic background check on each of the people they'd interviewed earlier in the day. One really grabbed her attention.

"Hey, Woody? How much do you know about the mayor?"

The chief shrugged. "He's up for re-election in November. Why?" He got up from the conference table and moved to stand behind her.

"It doesn't appear that Phineas Scott existed prior to 1997."

Chapter 9

"WHAT?" WOODY PEERED over PC's shoulder and looked at the computer screen. "That can't be right."

"But there it is." She moved the mouse around so the cursor circled a corner of Phineas Scott's birth certificate. "It says his birthday is April 1, 1972. But this is a much newer form. If you look in the bottom corner, it says, 'Form 18772 rev. 1995.'"

"Maybe it got lost, and he had to get a new one."

PC shook her head. "It would still be on the form used at the time he was born—it's got the doctor's signature, for one thing. Or should. He didn't apply for a Social Security card until 1997. Both are documents he needed to get a driver's license, which he also did in 1997. He would have been twenty-five. Seems a little old, but perhaps he was just a late bloomer."

Woody shrugged.

"How did he go to college, or get a job, or rent an apartment without any ID? Was he locked in his parents' basement or something? The hospital usually takes care of the birth certificate. Did someone just forget?"

"Could be he was born at home." Woody tried to shrug it off. "It's more common out in the country—a lot of rural counties don't even have hospitals."

"According to this birth certificate, he was born in Loving County, Texas."

Woody perked up. "That explains a lot. There's nothing out there but deer and cactus. I don't think two hundred people live in the whole county."

"What are you, the Texas Almanac?"

"I went to Sul Ross University in Alpine. Summers, I worked at Carlsbad Caverns, so I spent a lot of time in far west Texas and southeast New Mexico."

A tiny smile crept onto PC's lips. But it wasn't meant for Woody.

It was almost two decades ago, but it seemed like only last year. She and Mike had spent a three-day weekend at the Chisos Mountains Lodge in Big Bend National Park. Then they took the long way home, stopping at Carlsbad and Roswell before heading back into Texas for the Caverns of Sonora. After that, they made the nine-hour drive back to Houston in one long slog, only stopping in San Antonio to eat a late lunch.

The last night at Big Bend, they were supposed to be out looking for Perseid Meteors on the Lodge's observation deck. At least, that's what PC had thought they were doing. It was out under the Milky Way and a billion stars that Mike had proposed. He had a little flashlight to shine on the ring, and he was so nervous, he almost dropped it through a gap in the boardwalk when he took it out of the jewelry box.

"Donovan?"

PC startled. "Yeah. Loving County. Nearly vacant. Got it."

Woody's eyes fixed on her, apparently under the delusion that if he stared hard enough, he could see into her mind.

"It's almost 4:30. See if you can get it wrapped up by five, huh? But if you want to stay and look at some of those cold cases—off the clock, of course—feel free. I'm going back to my office."

"I'll see how it goes."

Woody paused at the doorway, and maybe it was just the way the fluorescent light spotlighted him against the wood door, but he looked unusually pale. He turned to ask, "Have you had any luck with that first one?"

"I'm sorry. What?"

"The binder I left in your car. When you first got to town? I figured you could really get your teeth into that one." He pushed the door open and left.

PC felt like she'd been punched in the gut. It was true. She'd found a copy of the case file of her father's murder on the front seat of her car while she'd been trying to get Rocky bailed out of jail. She'd guessed that Tran had smuggled it out to her, perhaps as a token of trust, but hadn't confronted him about it in case she was wrong.

I never suspected it was Woody.

Woody, who'd dumped her two nights before the Homecoming Dance. Woody, who didn't even come to her father's funeral. Were the files a peace offering, an attempt to help right a forty-year-old wrong?

It was hard to focus on the remaining report sections, and PC was glad that she'd been almost done when Woody casually dropped a hand grenade on his way out the door.

She'd gone out of her way to avoid him when she came to Possumwood in January. But when she had run into him, he was distant, and PC could feel an undercurrent of hostility. The detective had assumed it was because she was encroaching on his investigation into the Heather Micah murder. To her, clearing her brother was easily more important than Woody's pride. Her brain tried to turn Woody's motivations up, down, and around to examine them from every angle, as if they were some abstract sculpture.

FOCUS.

At last! She was done. 5:06. *Time to print and get out of here.*

PC followed the sound of the printer to the large machine in a bullpen workspace and collected it. Woody had stepped away, and she used his stapler before she left the reports on his desk. It was just as well. She wanted to ask him why he left her father's murder book in her car, but wasn't sure she was prepared for the answer. Besides, Mama's menagerie would be expecting dinner soon.

There was just enough time to get the critters fed—nothing like rattling a bucket of feed to make a girl feel appreciated—and let Cordite have a little romp before Rose served dinner.

After PC cleaned up and came into the dining room, she was a little surprised to see Terry Gillespie standing there.

He pulled out Rose's chair for her and she leaned her cheek against his hand on her shoulder after she sat down.

Back off, you old goat. "Mama, you sure you've healed up enough to be up and around cooking Sunday dinner?"

"Oh, honey. Of course, I am. Besides, I'm teaching Rocky how to cook—he did all the heavy liftin.'"

That might explain the grease spatters on his shirt.

PC went to the kitchen and served her own plate, as well as one for Rose. Rocky was almost done with his, piling it with fried chicken, green beans, and mashed potatoes.

"You cooked this? Looks pretty good."

"Nothin' to it." He gave her a half grin.

"Not when you got Mama standing over your shoulder, showing you what to do." PC picked up her own china. *Why did I have to say that? I should have just left it at "looks good."*

Nothing smells like fried chicken, or melted butter—it was just like all the Sundays she remembered growing up. PC skipped the green beans—Rose always added a generous dollop of bacon grease to almost everything, and the detective found that, after many years of not partaking, a little bit of that stuff went a long way.

The moment she put a bite of food in her mouth, Rose asked, "So, what did you get up to today?"

PC pointed to her mouth and exaggerated her chewing. She swallowed and said, "Just rode around with Woody and interviewed potential witnesses."

"Oooh!" Roses' eyes got big. "About the Azalea Trail murder?"

"It wasn't a murder. He died of an aortic aneurysm. But there is the question of how he came to be in Drew's shed."

"Very strange." Terry speared some green beans.

"It is, isn't it? But that's what the ME said. Haven't got the labs back yet, though."

"Who'd you talk to all day?" Rocky asked between mouthfuls of crispy chicken skin.

"The homeowners for this year's Azalea Trail. And Dinah Mae Brown."

Rose forced out a breath and rolled her eyes. "Dinah Mae. If brains were lard, she couldn't grease a pan."

"She's certainly very single-minded about the Historical Society." *What does Mama know, or think she knows, about Dinah Mae?*

"Oh, honey. She likes playing dress-up and taking credit for everything, but her assistant, Tess Meyer, does all the work. If Tess ever decides to go anywhere, The Mirabella Historical Society will fall apart." Rose scooped up some mashed potatoes.

Terry chuckled.

PC considered her water glass. *Hmmm. Wonder if Tess can shed any light on what Dinah Mae might have been doing after the meeting.* "Really, Mama? Why do you say that?"

"She's Scarlett O'Hara, without Sherman's March and a trail of dead husbands. At least, not as far as I know." She reached for a biscuit from the basket in the middle of the table. "How was work today, Rocky?"

They rambled on, small talk bouncing off PC's ears as she considered Dinah Mae. During the interview, the woman only had eyes for Woody. Was there an Ashley Wilkes or a Rhett Butler she had gone to dinner, or moved a body with after the Azalea Trail meeting?

This Sunday had felt like several Sundays seamed together, and PC was ready to collapse into bed. She stood in front of the bathroom mirror, brushing her teeth.

Dammit. I forgot to ask what time the IRS folks were coming in.

She glanced at her FlitBit. The knock-off fitness watch Daisy had bought her as a retirement present only displayed an icon of a broken battery.

Really? Didn't I just charge you a couple of days ago?

It had been 11:30 when she'd put down the three-ring binder that held the case file of her father's murder. She'd only been sixteen when he was killed, and while she still thought of him most days, details had dropped from her mind. PC had tried so hard to hold onto them, but sooner or later, they slipped through her fingers like water. She couldn't quite recall the sound of his voice, or the smell of his aftershave, but she would never forget the color of his eyes—they were the same green with gold flecks as the ones looking at her from the bathroom mirror.

Viewing the pictures of the crime scene had been harder than she'd thought it would be, but it got easier each time. PC was a detective. She'd seen many crime scenes. This was one of them. She pored over some section of the file each night, hoping to find that one missed clue that would crack the case. That was the best she could do, since it had happened forty years ago—most of the people who had any knowledge of the shooting were dead.

PC rinsed her toothbrush. She had to push the cold case to the back of her mind, let her subconscious percolate on it overnight; otherwise, she'd get no sleep.

It was probably too late to text Tran about the IRS agents, since he worked the day shift.

Of course! Cold case files. After she finished feeding the animals in the morning, she'd go to the station to have a look at some unsolved cases. What a coincidence, if the IRS people were there, too.

Annie was at the front desk when PC arrived in the lobby.

She smiled at the dispatcher. "Hey, girl. I just came by to work on some of those cold case files the Chief had mentioned." PC raised her commuter coffee cup.

"Sure thing. You know where the conference room is?"

"Yeah. I was there yesterday."

"Okay. I'll buzz you through."

"Thank you so much."

Once PC was behind the security door, she turned an ear toward Woody's office. Low voices drifted down the hallway. She went the long way to the conference room, passing by the Chief's office in a leisurely stroll.

"Donovan!" Woody called to her. "Come in here, please."

She stepped into the office and beamed, "Morning."

Woody's eyes narrowed for a moment. "This is Special Agent Shiro Faudi." He tilted his head to a thirty-ish female, who was wearing black slacks and a navy polo. "And this is Supervisory Special Agent Candice Newman." He gestured to a slim, middle-aged African American woman in a blue linen pantsuit and a crisp white blouse.

SSA Newman seemed familiar. *Of course.* "Thibaut Hebert, eight years ago."

"That's where I recognize you from, Detective Donovan. That was a great case, wasn't it? Good to see you again after all this time. Special Agent Faudi and I were at a training workshop in Georgia, and thunderstorms shut down the airport until early this morning. It sets me at ease to know you've been on the job here."

"Thank you. I'm very sorry about your colleague."

"Danvers was an outstanding agent. He will be missed."

Woody cleared his throat. "Donovan, I was going to ask if you'd assist the IRS staff in their investigation."

Of course you were. "I'd be delighted to." *And this will be on my invoice.*

"You can set them up in the conference room."

"Will do."

The two agents rose and followed PC down the hall. She pointed out the ladies' room and the miniscule break room on the way. The two women in blue set their laptops and other accouterments on the table.

"There's a water cooler and the copier/printer through there." PC motioned to the room across the hall.

"Thank you." SSA Newman picked up a file folder from the table. "You wrote these reports after interviewing potential witnesses yesterday. Is that correct?"

"Yes."

"Excellent. I'd like to—" Her phone rang, and she shook her head. "I'm sorry. I have to take this." She started walking toward the back of the conference room, finger in her free ear, and answered the phone.

PC turned to the other woman. "Agent Faudi, is there anything I can get for you?"

"Is there any coffee? And please, call me Shiro."

"I'll go check. Shiro."

If PC were to guess, she would think that the 'break room' had been labeled as 'closet' on the original building plans. There was a small counter with a sink, and she'd discovered it held cleaning supplies below, and coffee supplies in the upper cabinet. A mini-fridge hummed on the right side of the countertop and the coffeemaker, with about a half-inch of cold java in the carafe, perched on the left. At least the coffee machine wasn't one of the super-fancy ones that needed a degree in electrical engineering to operate. Filter in basket. Packet of coffee in filter. Rinse pot. Water in reservoir. Press START.

While she waited on the joe to brew, she scanned the bulletin board on the wall. It had all usual notices, OSHA, Labor Law, Heimlich Maneuver. A flyer for the Christmas party from four months ago. A picture of a shaggy black puppy with enormous, pointy ears.

The water gurgled up through the tubing. PC turned to verify that it was going where it was supposed to. It was. Mostly. Some of the hot liquid spattered out onto the counter.

Great.

Once the cycle finished, she wiped up the mess and poured a styro cup of perk-up juice before topping off her own travel mug. When she got back to the conference room, Shiro and Newman were talking quietly.

"I hope you like it black," PC announced as she entered.

"Yes. Yes, that will be fine."

The agents did not resume their conversation.

"Is everything all right?" PC took a sip of coffee.

Newman glanced at her colleague. "I have… a situation back in Houston. We picked up a rental at the airport, so we didn't have to go all the way back downtown. Now Agent Faudi is going to have to drive me back to Houston and come all the way back out here. She'll lose hours of case time."

"Oh… I can take you. I've got a couple of things I need to do in town, anyway. It's no problem. Really."

Newman regarded PC while she took a few moments, apparently reviewing her options.

"Yes. I think that'll work."

"I'll let Wo- the Chief know where we're going and I'll meet you out front." PC turned to Shiro. "He can help you with whatever you need."

"Thank you, Detective."

PC waved goodbye to Annie as she left, then pulled out her phone and dialed Rose before she unlocked the car door.

"Hey, Mama. I had something come up and I have to go to Houston. Do you need anything while I'm there?"

"Not that—actually, yes. Could you get some mangoes and kiwi fruit?"

"Sure."

Newman came out and looked around. PC waved. "I gotta go, Mama. I'll talk to you soon."

Now, with Supervisory Special Agent Newman as her captive audience, perhaps she'd finally get some answers.

Chapter 10

SSA Newman got into PC's car. "I'm sure you're dying to ask who Danvers was surveilling."

PC's ears pricked up, and she backed out of the parking space.

"We have a policy. We don't share information until after we've made an indictment. That's when we update the N-DEx database, because we know other agencies might be investigating the same individual. But a leak could cripple our investigation."

Before she could argue, or rather, negotiate, a thought popped into her head. *What if Mama's friend, Justice, was the 'Justice' of the note found with Danvers' body?*

Did she really want to know?

But PC shook it off and considered her options. She didn't want to jeopardize the good will she'd earned with SSA Newman on that Thibaut case. But IRS Special Agents aren't the ones coming after people who neglected to file their taxes last year. They investigate money laundering, embezzlement, and credit card fraud, to name a few. It was the IRS who took down Al Capone, after all. They don't play around. If there was something going on, it was major. Was it anybody she knew?

On the other hand, Agent Faudi was going to be in Possumwood for however long it took to wrap up the investigation. And PC would be helping her. There was no way she could keep *everything* secret, was there?

PC sighed resignedly, mostly for effect. "I thought you might say something like that." She turned on to Justice Avenue, headed for the 720 Loop to get out of town. "So, where am I dropping you?"

"Smith."

Mickey Leland Federal Building on Smith Street, downtown. Good. That's probably the closest office to my house. "Got it."

The two women made sporadic small talk until the journey's end. They said their goodbyes and PC watched Newman walk into the sleek glass and steel tower. The lunch rush was going to start at any moment, and PC wanted to be out of downtown before the onslaught.

She was missing her favorite hole-in-the wall TexMex, and she probably had just enough time to get there before the line started. She took the Studemont exit off of I-10 and rolled into the Heights. Her Craftsman bungalow had been very affordable back in the early 90s, before gentrification crept in. Now, prices were obscene, and she was constantly getting letters from realtors trying to coax her into selling. How many business cards would be tucked into her screen door today?

Century-old restored Victorians were interspersed with 1960s Craftsmans, twenty-first century faux lofts, and Victorian-inspired duplexes. Pocket parks squeezed in between businesses that were located both in strip centers and re-purposed houses. Some lots were tiny, some were huge, and most overflowed with plants. Live oaks, some of which were saplings when the Victorians were built, lined the streets. In yards, fruit trees were popular, especially peaches and citruses. Pink flowered peaches and white flowered plums were just reaching their peaks, and it wouldn't be long before the homeowners were battling squirrels to keep at least some of their luscious harvests. In a few months, when heat and humidity became almost unbearable, crepe myrtles in whites, pinks, reds, and purples would burst into bloom, their flowers smelling like sweet, fresh hay.

The light changed, and PC turned onto West 11th. *Great! Still some parking spaces.*

The sign towered over the inadequate parking lot. Hot pink, garish orange, and radioactive green neon lights had been replaced several years ago with even brighter LED lights, those same colors throbbing and chasing each other around a bright white 'Hermano de Felix.' A handful of wrought-iron tables and chairs lurked behind the banana trees that crowded the brick-lined flower beds, which the strip center designer had probably intended for seasonal color annuals. The faux thatched awning was presumably meant as a Yucatan resort-style flourish. Two relentlessly colorful Talavera lizards clung to the concrete walls, guarding the front door.

PC opened it and went inside.

The air was cool, and the large, tinted windows muted the incoming sunlight. Corn tortillas perfumed the air. It was just as she remembered it.

"Detective! We haven't seen you in a while."

"I know, Maria. It's been too long. I've been out of town, taking care of my mother."

"Ah. Are you back home now?" Maria picked up a menu and started toward the dining area.

"Possibly end of the month. Depends on what her doctor says."

"It's good to see you." Maria's eyes turned toward the opening door. She set the menu down and hurried away to seat the next customers.

Before PC had completely settled in, a server arrived with a basket of warm tortilla chips and a dish of fire-roasted red pepper salsa.

"Hey, stranger. You having your usual?"

"Yeah, I am, Carmela. Been craving that chile relleno. Nobody makes it like your mom."

The waitress smiled. "She knows."

A few minutes later, Carmela brought a glass of iced tea, but PC barely noticed. She'd taken out her notebook and was reviewing her notes from yesterday's interview extravaganza, grazing on chips and smoky, chunky salsa.

The biggest questions she had were:

Where was Joe Watkins between 8:30 and midnight?

Who pulled up in the Watkins' driveway at 9:00?

Where/who was Phineas Scott prior to 1997?

Who or what did "Justice" mean?

If PC was investigating a money laundering operation, the person who seemingly materialized out of nowhere would be her primary subject. But she'd have to see who Agent Faudi wanted to look into first.

There was a good chance, given both his reputation and evasiveness, that Joe had a girlfriend somewhere, who may or may not be Dinah Mae Brown, and that is where his missing time went. Who knows, perhaps Amanda had her own side piece, and that explains the 9 PM headlights. But that was just speculation—there was no evidence. It could also be true that they set up their spat to provide a cover story, Joe picked Amanda up, and they interacted with Agent Danvers, then stashed him in Drew's shed when things went sideways. Maybe Joe was out disposing of Danvers' personal effects until midnight.

"Hot plate."

A young man held out an oval platter with his napkin- wrapped hand, and PC moved her notebook out of the way so he could set it down.

"Thanks." She'd forgotten how fast they got the food out here.

PC breathed in and savored the aromas coming off her steaming plate. Two narrow peppers, almost as long as her hand and stuffed with Fernanda's above-top-secret blend of cheeses and spices, then breaded and deep-fried, floated in a central pool of mole sauce. A zig-zag drizzle of sour cream adorned the tops. Yellow rice piled onto one side of the plate, while re-fried beans and a generous scoop of guacamole filled the other.

Her fork crunched through the top layer and cut the tender pepper below, then brought the decadent morsel up to her mouth. It was easy to get chile relleno wrong, and end up with a sad, greasy sponge embracing a limp pepper. But not here. Not ever.

What would Drew think of this place? Would he ever come and visit her? Was he being investigated by the IRS?

That last thought put a damper on her mood. She finished her lunch, paid her check, and headed to her house.

As she pulled into the driveway, a man in a business suit stepped out onto the concrete porch of her next-door neighbor's house. He pulled the brim of his cowboy hat down as he checked the street before hurrying to the Lexus parked in front of the house and driving away.

He had barely left the curb when PC's neighbor, Robin Valone, came out, wearing gardening gloves and carrying a hand pruner. She waved a daisy print covered hand.

PC had an alarm system, but she still asked her neighbors, Robin to the left and Sam and Janet Evensong to the right, to keep an eye on her house for her. It was good to see one of them out and about.

Robin adjusted her wide-brimmed hat and strolled over. "Hey, PC. How's your mother?" Ms. Valone was only a few years younger than PC, and very fit.

"She seems to be doing well. I guess we'll find out at the end of the month."

"I'm so glad to hear that." Robin smiled and surreptitiously took in a deep breath. "I know it's a big ask. And I won't be mad if you say 'no,' but my niece, Felicity, just got an offer for a summer research fellowship downtown. She's moving from Arizona, just finished her bachelor's at Christmas. She'll be starting at Rice in the fall to get her Master's in Computer Science. The thing is…"

Please get on with it.

"She doesn't want to accept the fellowship offer unless she can find a place to live. There is absolutely nothing available, at least nothing she can afford, anywhere near downtown or the Medical Center. She's on the waitlist for campus housing in the fall, but she'll probably get in."

"And you're wondering if I'd rent my house to her?"

"Oh! Not your whole house. Just a room. Until she finds a place of her own."

PC fidgeted with her keys. "And she can't stay with you?"

Robin raised an eyebrow. "With my business?"

Very, very few of the neighbors knew that Robin was a full-time dominatrix, and men paid her obscene sums to insult them while they cleaned her house and did her laundry wearing nothing but a few strips of leather and latex. She also provided a similar, internet-based service.

"Good point. Let me think about it. When was she looking to move in?"

"The fellowship starts June first. But she has a job as an online tutor. If you wanted her to house sit for you while you're away…?"

"She sounds very smart and resourceful, but I'd like to meet her before I commit."

Robin gave a quick, bird-like nod. "Of course. I would expect that. Yes. I can set up an on-line meeting, if you want."

"Like I said, let me think about it. When does she need an answer?"

"The deadline to accept the fellowship is March 31."

"I'll let you know before then."

"Thanks, PC. I appreciate that more than you know."

"It was good seeing you, but I've got to get back to Possumwood soon. I'm just going to have a look around and make sure everything's in order."

Robin went back to her gardening, and PC checked the mailbox. Her mail was forwarded to Rose's, but she still occasionally got grocery circulars and other junk mail. A cloud of oak pollen puffed into the air as she opened it, and PC sneezed. Today, the mailbox was empty. Too bad—she was hoping for some junk mail to wipe her hand post-sneeze. She climbed the three concrete steps to her wide front porch, then picked through her keys. Six business cards from realtors spilled onto the porch as the door and jamb parted company. She scooped them up and dumped them into the recycling bin inside the front door.

The air was close and had that almost-musty smell of a house that's been shut up for a while. She opened the back windows and turned the ceiling fan up to high to move the air around faster. The HVAC had a smart thermostat, so that the heat came on if it was colder than 40, and the AC came on if it was hotter than 82. PC had to keep the black mold, which thrived on heat and damp, at bay—otherwise she'd have to pay for remediation, and that was a budget buster.

The back yard was nearly at the point a machete was necessary, but she didn't have time today. She tried to come home at least once a week, but didn't always make it. The Evensongs paid their lawn crew extra to cut PC's front grass when they did their weekly rounds, and PC paid Sam up front at the beginning of the month. But nobody went into the back yard. The space looked naked without Cordite, although PC was concerned he might get lost in that tall grass, or grabbed by the rampant mustang grape vine that was holding her hydrangea hostage. Perhaps she could recruit Rocky to help her next week.

Or Drew.

If he wasn't in jail for money laundering.

PC continued her rounds, flushing both toilets and letting each faucet run for a minute or so. The FlitBit caught on the towel rack in the master bath, and she noticed it was almost 1:30.

I gotta get back. Agent Faudi will probably need my help.

She shut the house up and was just getting in the car when her phone rang.

"Hey, Tran. What's up?"

"There's been an accident."

Chapter 11

"WHAT HAPPENED?" PC asked, then connected her phone to the car's Bluetooth.

Tran's voice was momentarily interrupted by static. "Agent Faudi was driving out in the area of the Quenton Plantation when she hit a feral hog. Tried to swerve, but didn't quite make it and rolled the car. With that low center of gravity, hitting a pig is like hitting a brick wall. Anyway, last report I heard, she was critical, but stable. She's a mess, though. They Life Flighted her back to Houston—Hermann Hospital, and she'll probably be in surgery for hours."

"Did you call Agent Newman yet?"

"I left a message. Apparently, she's on a plane, but they didn't say where she was headed."

PC slumped back in her seat. "I'll stop by the hospital and see if there are any updates."

By the time PC got to the Texas Medical Center, traffic was starting to build. Not bad yet, but it wouldn't be long. TMC was a rabbit's warren of towering glass and steel hospitals, doctors' offices, and hotels that sprawled across many city blocks. It was bounded on the northwest by Rice University, the northeast by Hermann park (zoo, golf course, and amphitheater handy for patients' family members). To the south lay the rotting hulk of the former 8th Wonder of the World, the Astrodome, and its high-tech replacement, NRG Stadium. A westward track led to some very tony neighborhoods, while the houses to the east were… somewhat less tony.

She wondered if she had any string or breadcrumbs to leave a trail as she drove around the labyrinthine parking garage. PC didn't need to ask where the trauma center waiting room was. She remembered. Her hands shook as she reached for the elevator button, and a wave of nausea passed over her. She stepped into the elevator with a handful of other people and tried to breathe deeply to let the emotion pass.

Once she got up to the trauma surgery waiting room, she studied the occupants. There was a group of three, two women and a man; a middle-aged couple; and a youngish man in a navy suit, typing on a laptop. She approached the solitary man.

"Excuse me? Are you by any chance with the IRS?"

He stopped tapping and looked up. "Why do you ask?"

She'd better sound as official as possible. "I'm Detective Sergeant Donovan. I was working with Agent Faudi in Possumwood, and I was told she'd been in an accident."

He scrutinized her face for some seconds.

If he asks to see my badge, I'm toast.

"Yes." He dipped his head toward the seat beside him.

PC sat. "Are there any updates on her condition?"

The man rubbed the bridge of his nose. "No. They're trying to put her face back together—hopefully the bone fragments aren't too small. It's going to take some time."

Under other conditions, PC would have waited with the unnamed agent. But she had to get back to Possumwood. She still had some old business cards in her bag, as well as pens and a small notebook, so she took out a card and scratched through her former business number and wrote her cell number beneath it.

PC held the card out to the man. "As soon as you hear anything, please give me a call, Agent…?"

He took the card. "Smalley." Then tucked it into his computer case. "I'll do that."

"Thanks. I only just met her this morning. I really hope they're able to get her patched up."

"Me too. Thank you for stopping by." He returned to tapping on the keys.

Dismissed, PC made her way back out to the parking garage. The elevator door opened.

Crap. Am I on the orange level or the yellow?

The elevator car was filling up. She picked orange. She was wrong. After scouring both the orange and yellow levels, fear began to rise in her chest. Had her car been stolen? Towed? Or was she just on the wrong floor? She ran up two flights of stairs to the red level, and there it was, waiting patiently for her.

Next time, take one of the little cards by the elevator and avoid this nonsense. You know you always freak out at hospitals.

Gratefully, PC slipped behind the wheel and started the drive back to Possumwood. She didn't have nearly enough pieces to solve the Pete Danvers puzzle, so she listened to a couple of episodes of a true crime podcast. Maybe she'd get some ideas.

PC was about fifteen minutes away from Possumwood when her phone rang. She tapped a button on the console and answered. "Hey, Tran." There was a lot of background noise.

"Any word on Faudi?"

"No. She was still in surgery. I gave my card to an agent in the waiting area and told him to call me as soon as there was any news."

"Well, I hope she'll be okay. Listen, I wanted to tell you the rental car company was able to track Danvers' car. Someone drove it off the boat ramp at Mirabella State Park. We got some divers from DPS, and it's being winched out now."

"I'll be there in about twenty minutes." She hung up.

Now maybe we'll get somewhere.

PC hoped all the state troopers in the area were busy at the lake, because her foot was heavy on the gas all the way to the park entrance. The detective had to fling her right hand out several times to prevent Rose's mangoes from rolling onto the floor. She drove through an open wrought-iron gate and saw the entry control hut just ahead.

The ranger leaned out the window as she pulled up, a parking garage arm blocking her way.

"Day camping for one?" he asked, giving her car a quick scan.

"Actually, I'm here with the PPD. They're pulling a car out of the lake…"

"ID?"

"I, uh, just have my regular license. But Officer Tran called me to come. I can give him a call and you can speak to him."

"I'm sorry. Without official ID, I still need the six dollars."

Daylight was burning. She didn't want to waste another second arguing with the ranger. She pulled out a ten-dollar bill and handed it over. The ranger handed her four crisp ones, a map of the park, and a receipt with scotch tape on it.

"Place that in your window. Usually just above your inspection sticker works well. Thank you and enjoy your stay. Gates close at ten."

The ranger raised the flimsy gate and PC started to shift into drive.

"Excuse me, sir?"

The ranger poked his head back out the window. "Yes?"

"Do you have any security cameras in the park?"

"Just that one," he looked up and PC followed his eyes to a black half-sphere under the eave. "And the one at the nature center."

"Have they already asked you to pull video from this camera?"

"No."

"The person who dumped the car probably did it Thursday night or early Friday morning, but it could have happened later in the week. What time does the gate open in the morning?"

"Six AM."

"I see. Could you pull that feed from Thursday evening through this morning and send it to Chief Wilson?"

"IT guy'll need a form."

"I'll send it when I get back to the station."

PC followed the signs to the boat launch area. As she got opened her door, she could see they were decoupling a white Hyundai Elantra from the winch truck. A strand of green pondweed hung from an Alabama license plate. Tran stood near the bank, so she made her way over. They watched as water streamed out of the car. When the flow had slowed to a drip, one of the state troopers opened the driver's side door. All the windows had been rolled down, probably to help it fill with water faster. A small catfish flopped on the floorboard, and the trooper tossed it back into the lake.

A young man in a red polo and khaki slacks tapped on a tablet computer while he spoke on his phone via a headset.

"Yeah. Total loss… Doing the insurance claim right now."

He must be from the rental company.

Tran handed PC a pair of gloves as they approached the vehicle. She opened the front passenger door, and he opened the rear one.

Danvers' waterlogged laptop lay haphazardly on the back seat. "Hope he had a cloud backup." Tran looked down.

An open suitcase, contents scattered either by a ransacking or water, glistened next to the ruined computer.

The rental car keys were in the ignition. A ring with several keys on it lay on the passenger floorboard. Next to that was a bright orange lid that looked like it might have come off a glue stick, although it was narrower and arched. Another bit of orange plastic peeked out from underneath the seat. Danvers' Best Southern hotel room key, on its gaudy orange fob.

"What is this?" Tran asked.

PC looked through the gap between the front seats. "I think it's an owl." *It looks like the white glass one at Drew's gallery.* "We should get all of these items photographed. You got the markers?"

"Yeah. I'll get them out of the trunk." He headed toward his squad.

What am I going to do? I'd better check for myself if that owl is still sitting by Drew's cash register. If not... She didn't want to think about that option.

Possumwood PD didn't have enough crime to justify employing a full-time crime scene photographer, so the officers took their own photos. Tran came back and handed PC a stack of yellow evidence markers. She placed one by each item in the car, and he took pictures.

"Make sure you get shots from multiple angles and get close-ups of the tire treads."

A shadow fell across her face, and PC looked up. One of the DPS troopers stood there, blotting out the sun. She guessed he was at least 6'6" and built like a tank.

"How's it going?" he asked.

PC shrugged. "Okay, I guess. Couple of things I can't explain, but everything else looks like what you'd expect to find when somebody's trying to hide evidence."

"Oh?"

"Yeah. I don't know why this little glass owl is in the car. Or this weird orange lid."

He peered into that car at both objects. "Well, I can't tell you anything about the owl, but your decedent must have had food allergies. That lid's from an epinephrine injector—you know, like an EpiPen? My little boy has a peanut allergy, so we always have them around."

"I did not know that. Thanks. Hope your son stays safe."

He nodded and wandered off toward the winch truck.

Now that's an interesting thing to know. Did this cap come from Danvers' injector, or did it belong to the person who stashed his body?

She gathered up some paper evidence bags and started labeling them with the marker number, location, and contents.

The door to The Best Little Art Gallery in Texas was locked, but PC could see Drew moving around the lobby. She tapped on the glass, and he stopped what he was doing.

The deadbolt clanked as Drew opened the door. "Hey, PC. Come on in." Salt and pepper stubble shaded his cheeks.

"I wanted to stop by and see how you're doing." *That is true. But it isn't the only reason.*

He rubbed his bristly chin. "Overslept this morning, didn't have time to shave."

PC nodded. "It happens."

"You care for anything to drink?"

"Some cold water'd be great."

He stepped behind the counter. A mini fridge purred underneath it, and he retrieved two bottles of water.

As he handed one over to her, he said, "Got some grapes, too. And some smoked Gouda."

"Thanks, but I'm good. I just wanted to see how you were doing. I didn't want to keep you here at work. You're probably more than ready to get home."

She checked three times. Then once more for good measure. The owl figurine wasn't on the counter.

Chapter 12

DREW KNIT HIS brows. "PC? Is something wrong? You look pale all of a sudden."

"Oh. I'm fine. Just tired—it's been a long day." She turned her eyes to the cash register. "Oh. It's gone."

Drew opened his own water bottle. "What's that?"

PC languidly drew her finger across the marble countertop and stopped where she remembered seeing the glass knickknack. "I had noticed you had a little owl figurine, and I thought it was cool. I was going to ask you about it, but you seem to have sold it."

"Huh. I didn't realize you were interested in Depression glass. That one's a Westmoreland milk glass toothpick holder. People were crazy about owls back in the day—Westmoreland produced a ton of them, and… I'm sorry. You weren't looking for Antiques Roadshow. I was bringing in some new paintings for our next exhibit and I knocked it off the counter. One of the wings broke, and I gave it to Amanda on Thursday evening. She said she'd take it back to the shop and fix it."

I'll definitely check that out. But not tonight. "Where else would you send an antique to be repaired, except for an antique shop? Right?"

"Especially when that's where you bought it." He crossed his arms. "Are you sure there's nothing you want to tell me?"

PC took a sip of water. "Are you aware that the IRS is out here investigating after Special Agent Danvers was found in your shed?"

"Yes."

"Did you hear about the accident out by Quenton Plantation this afternoon?"

"No."

"Well, the agent that was picking up the case was in a bad car accident near the plantation. They had to Life Flight her to The Medical Center."

"Oh, wow." He touched her shoulder. "I'm really sorry to hear that. Is there anything I can do?"

PC shook her head. "Thanks, but I have to go. Mama's menagerie is probably already agitating for their dinner. I'm a bit behind schedule."

"Well, keep me posted. If there's any way I can help, just ask. I mean that."

"Thanks." She gave the counter a final glance before turning away from Drew.

Her heart was heavy as she trudged out the door. The owl that Tran found in the car had not appeared to have been damaged in any way. What possible reason would Drew's owl be in Danvers' car. Danvers was a kleptomaniac? Danvers grabbed it as a way to point to Drew as his killer? There had better be an owl with a broken wing at Vintage Glory antiques.

When PC got to Rose's house, she was not in the mood to talk to anyone. She dropped her bag and car keys onto a chair on the back porch. The smell of spaghetti sauce wafted out, and it didn't even make her hungry. Cordite yipped at the screen door, so she let him out to supervise the nightly critter feeding.

She had just gathered the eggs and locked the chicken coop when Rocky stuck his head out the door. "Dinner's ready."

"Go ahead without me. I'll be here a while."

He disappeared back inside. Once the feed was doled out, and Hazel, Guinevere, and Arthur were happily munching away instead of complaining at her, mucking the pen gave her time to think. If the man that Ada and Phineas saw was indeed Pete Danvers, was Ada the person he was trying to call? Dinah had said that Ada's phone kept going off during the meeting. Phineas left to take a call—could it have been Danvers? Don was fifteen minutes late—plenty of time for a call. The Watkinses both left at separate times, and neither one had a good alibi—was Danvers the one who pulled into their driveway at 9:00? What if Joe met Danvers at the Biersal—no one else seemed to have gone there. Shame they were closed on Mondays, or she would already have been down to chat with the bartender. Was Danvers investigating more than one person? Maybe several folks had a reason to want him dead.

Another scoop of poop on the pile for Justice. *Hope that mushroom business is taking off for her.*

What did that slip of paper mean, anyway? Justice the concept? Justice the friend? One of the Justice businesses on Justice Avenue? It made her head spin. Why was there an epinephrine injector cap in Danvers' car?

PC's phone vibrated in her pocket. She wiped her hands on her thighs, knowing that wouldn't get them nearly clean enough to touch the screen, and answered it.

"Detective Sergeant Donovan?"

"Yes?"

"This is Agent Smalley. I just wanted to let you know that Agent Faudi is out of surgery. She's critical, but stable. And she's on a lot of medication, so she's not really... lucid."

"Thanks for the update. At least it's not bad news. Keep me posted, okay? We're all pulling for her out here."

"Will do." He clicked off without a goodbye.

The pitchfork awaited her, though she was almost done. At last, the final scoop was on the pile. PC pushed her musings to the back burner so they could simmer over night.

The cowbells on the front door clanged as PC opened it.

"Good morning!" chirped the perky cashier. "Welcome to Dot's Fine Wines and Liquors. Is there something in particular that you're looking for?"

"Yes. Ada Dotson. Is she in?"

"And who may I tell her is here?"

"PC Donovan."

The young woman picked up the receiver on a clunky desk phone and pressed a button.

"Ms. Dotson, there's a PC Donovan here to see you... I don't know... Okay."

"If you go through those double doors," the cashier pointed to the back of the store, "you'll see a sign that says 'Office' on your left."

"Thanks."

PC made her way down an aisle of Spanish and Italian red wine, then saw the doors in the back corner. She pulled one open and went into the warehouse section of the store. A forest of wooden crates, a walk-in cooler, and pallets of beer cases loomed to her right. A water heater, HVAC equipment, and an electrical box took up a large portion of the left wall. The office was built out from the wall, an afterthought with thick plywood that didn't quite reach the ceiling. Pink insulation peeked out over the tops, and a silver ventilation duct attached its mouth to the center of the office's ceiling, the other end disappearing off to the right. She knocked on the door.

"Come in."

"Morning, Ms. Dotson."

"Ada."

"Ada. I had a couple more questions to ask you, if you have a minute?"

"Sure." She gestured to one of the metal chairs in front of her desk.

PC sat and got out her notebook. "So, first of all, Dinah Mae Brown said that you got several calls throughout the meeting. I was wondering who was calling."

Ada let out a huge sigh. "It was my sister in Dallas. My nephew is going through… a rebellious phase. He got arrested shoplifting, and she wanted me to send her some bail money. His name is Billy Burke, if you want to confirm."

"Thanks. Did you send her the money?"

"I did, but told her to let him spend the night in jail. Might scare him straight."

PC Nodded. "Might do. The second question: You and Phineas Scott walked home from Mr. Burlesconi's house, correct?"

"Yes."

"The mayor said there was a man in the employee parking lot at the Little Gallery who waved at the two of you. Did you know him?"

"I think so. It was dark, but he kinda looked like the man who came in to make a special order of Australian Sagranito. I could get Italian, and there are a limited number of domestic vintners for that wine, so I asked if he'd like to try one of those instead. He said sure, and I ordered a case of Italian for him. Picked it up Thursday morning."

"And do you remember his name?"

"After all of that paperwork? Of course. Pete Danvers."

Was this a work purchase, or did he just like uncommon wine?

"How did he pay for it?"

"Cash. We offer a 10% discount for cash sales, and a lot of our customers take advantage of it."

PC closed her notebook and stood up. "Thank you, Ms.—Ada. I appreciate your time."

She showed herself out and got in her car, mentally moving Ada to the bottom of her Persons of Interest list. May as well head down to the station and check for new developments.

"Hey, Annie." PC smiled at the dispatcher.

"I didn't realize you were working today."

"Yeah, well, I thought I'd come by and see if there were any updates on the Danvers case. And have a look at some of the cold cases."

"Sure. I'll buzz you in."

"Thanks."

PC walked through the security door and down the hall toward the conference room. As she passed the break closet, she noticed Woody in there, one hand clutching his abdomen and the other pressed against the wall.

"You okay, Chief?"

"Yep." He grimaced. "Really queasy. I think the coffee creamer may be out of date or something…'cause my gut's sure reacting to it."

"Mama always said if you had an upset stomach, a fizzy drink would either settle it or make what's ailing you bubble up and out. Why don't you sit down? I'll get you something. Any ginger ale in the machine?"

"Don't think so. It'll pass. It always does."

That doesn't sound like bad coffee creamer. "I'm sorry you had a bad reaction."

Woody straightened, but his jaw was still clenched. "Thanks."

PC didn't even hear him. Something had bubbled to the top of that clue stew simmering on the back burner. *A… bad… reaction.*

"Chief? I don't think Pete Danvers died of natural causes. I think he was murdered."

Chapter 13

WOODY SCOWLED. "THAT'S not what the autopsy report said." He dropped his hand from his stomach down to his side.

"Can we go to your office and get Dr. Mack on the phone?" PC asked.

Woody was pale as biscuit dough and didn't look like he had much fight in him. "Sure. I was going to sit down, anyway."

They got to his office, and he sank into the pleather chair behind his desk. She perched on one of the scratched chrome and Naugahyde seats that was probably new in the 1970s. Woody fumbled with his phone.

Good grief! How long does it take you to get to the Cs in your contact list?

Woody finally found the number on his cell and tapped the screen, then switched it to speaker mode.

"Hey, Chief. What can I do you for?"

"Dr. Mack? Detective Sergeant Donovan wanted to talk to you about the Danvers case. She thinks it's murder."

PC could hear the eye roll in his voice.

"He died of an aneurysm. Not sure how a murderer could have accomplished that."

PC leaned toward the phone. "Danvers was on heart medication. We found a lid from an epinephrine injector on the floor of his car. I'm thinking maybe there was a drug interaction?"

"Do you know what the medication was?" The sound of pages turning crackled over the speaker. "I don't have it in my notes."

"It was in his hotel room. Started with a 'T' and it was for arrythmia. Let me get my notebook."

Dr. Mack paused for a minute. "Maybe Tambocor? My wife takes that."

She found the page she was looking for. "Yes, that's it."

"Somebody with a heart condition shouldn't take epinephrine, but I don't think there'd be a drug interaction."

PC slumped against the vinyl.

"However." Dr. Mack stopped, presumably gathering his thoughts. "Epinephrine does cause a spike in blood pressure, could be enough to blow out a weakened aneurysm. Also, it can cause an arrythmia, so if he already had that condition, somebody *could* have been trying to force an episode. People have fatal arrhythmias every day."

"Is that something that will show up in the labs?"

"There is no post-mortem test for arrythmia—if the heart's not beating, it has no rhythm, normal or otherwise. Epinephrine isn't usually something we test for, and it doesn't persist long in samples. I can ask the lab to add catecholamine blood and urine tests, but I can't promise the compounds will still be there, even if he was injected."

"Thanks, Dr. Mack. I appreciate that."

Woody's chair squealed as he bent toward his smartphone. "Would you be able to find a mark on the body from the injection?"

"It depends. If Mr. Danvers sat calmly and quietly, then it would be pretty much impossible. But if he was struggling, there might be some bruising or a scratch from the needle. The problem is, his body's already been shipped back to his next of kin in Houston. I can review my report and the photos we took during the autopsy, though."

"That would be amazing. Thanks!" PC was on the right track. She could feel it in her bones.

"Anything else y'all need?"

PC grinned. "That's all I had in mind. Thanks for hearing me out."

"Let us know what you find out, Dr. Mack." Woody ended the call, then looked up at PC. "Don't take this the wrong way, but until I hear from Dr. Mack, I'm not opening a homicide investigation."

"I understand. You sure I can't get you anything?"

He cleared his throat and swallowed a few times. "I'm fine. Don't you have some cold case files to look at or something?"

"Indeed." PC got up and made her way to the conference room. If Woody was still even half as hard-headed as he used to be, he'd be passed out on the floor, half dead before he would let anyone help him.

She dragged one of the banker's boxes off the bookshelf and pulled out the first file.

Over an hour passed, and she hadn't seen anything in the files that looked promising. Her stomach rumbled, and she thought it might be a logical time to go to lunch. She had just started to tidy up the files she'd been looking at when her phone vibrated.

It was a text from Woody. One word. *Office.*

PC tapped the file folder on the desk to settle the papers, then put everything away and obeyed the summons.

Woody was leaning back in his chair, talking on his phone. She hovered in the doorway.

"… yeah…. Why is that?… I see… okay… okay… thanks, doc." He hung up and looked at PC, without bothering to ask her to come in and sit.

"Dr. Mack said after scouring all the photos and reports, he had noted a tiny scratch and a small bruise at the base of Danvers' throat, just above his collarbone."

"I see." *I knew it!*

"I'm going to re-open this case as a possible homicide. Since you've been collaborating with Tran anyway, why don't you two look into it?"

PC nodded and looked at him expectantly.

He sighed. "Yeah. You're on the payroll. You sure generate a lot of invoices, for someone who's supposed to be retired," he grumbled.

"I'll text Tran."

The lunch crowd at *Jillibella's Mexican Cantina* was starting to build. PC had gone to school with the owner, Jill, and that's how she knew the fabricated name was pronounced JIL-ee-BEL-a, rather than the Spanish pronunciation of that collection of letters— HEE-ee-bay-ah.

She and Tran were seated, and they picked up big, laminated menus. There were the expected TexMex items, like queso dip, burritos, and flour tortillas.

A waiter with a skillet of sizzling fajitas walked past, thick steam billowing off the grilled meat and onions.

Their own server came by with a basket of tortilla chips and a dish of salsa.

"Do y'all need a minute, or do you know what you want?"

"I'll have water, and whatever the lunch special is." Tran closed his menu and handed it to her.

"I'll have the…" PC made a frantic scan down the shiny inside pages. "Acapulco Platter, please."

"Refried beans or black?"

"Black. And iced tea."

"Got it. I'll have those drinks out in a minute."

PC picked up a chip and dipped it in the sauce. It was a lot better than she was expecting—chunks of roasted jalapeno peppers and tomatoes bathed in a thick tomato sauce rich with cumin and coriander. She'd have to be careful—she could eat the whole basket of chips just to get at the sauce.

While they were waiting, she pulled out her notebook, and filled Tran in on everything she knew so far.

The meal came and went, spicy, cheesy morsels disappearing under the discussion of ominous motives. When the plates were cleared and the checks were paid, Tran leaned back in the booth. "I should have gotten coffee. After all that food, I need a nap."

"Sorry. No rest for the weary. I was thinking we could go find Don Weingarten—I have a couple of questions I'd like to ask him. I don't think he or his wife had anything to do with it, but he might know who does, even if he doesn't realize it."

Tran drove the short distance to the Weingarten's palatial home. They got out and walked up the brick path to toward the front door, the marble lions marking their passing. Don stood in a corner of the front yard, dead-heading a white rosebush.

"Good afternoon, Mr. Weingarten!" PC put on her best cheerful smile.

"Oh, it's you. Detective... Donigan?"

"Donovan. I just had a couple of quick questions I wanted to ask, if you have a minute?"

He shrugged, then continued clipping off the spent blooms. "Sure."

Tran stood slightly behind PC, more of an accessory than anything else.

"Great. First of all, do you or your wife have any food allergies?"

The snipping stopped. "I'm sorry?"

"Food allergies. You know, like you eat peanuts and your throat closes up?"

"Why are you asking this?"

Tran coughed.

PC leaned forward, just a little, and spoke in a low, conspiratorial voice. "I can't tell you the details, for obvious reasons, but we suspect the killer might be someone with severe allergies. We found one piece of evidence, but we think there's more at the Burlesconi residence."

"Killer? I had heard it was natural causes—a heart attack or something."

PC's eyebrows raised. "Or something."

Gobsmacked, Weingarten's mouth fell open, and he closed it with a snap. "No. Neither of us have any allergies. Well, dairy sometimes gives Sofia indigestion, but other than that, nothing."

"Would you by any chance know if one of the people at Thursday night's meeting has any severe allergies?"

"I don't think so, but I've never really asked."

"Thanks, anyway."

"Of-of course." *Snip. Snip.* Withered blossoms fell.

"Now, there's one other thing. You said your wife's Mercedes broke down. Where do you take a car like that to get it fixed around here?"

"You have to go to Clovis Luxury Car in Horice, it's about twenty minutes north on 720."

I know where it is. "Thank you for your time, Mr. Weingarten. You have a nice afternoon, now."

"I will."

PC turned and strolled down the path, Tran following her like a toy on a string. As soon as the car doors were closed, he frowned.

"Why did you tell him about the injector? He's not going to keep that to himself."

"Of course, he isn't. With any luck, he's going to tell everybody he knows. And they'll tell their friends… and hopefully the person who thinks they got rid of all the evidence will come looking for the piece they missed."

"And we just have to see who shows up."

"Exactly. Now, I need to talk to Amanda Watkins about an owl."

Chapter 14

THE DOOR TO Vintage Glory Antiques chimed as PC and Tran entered. No one was at the counter. Or in the aisles.

"Hello?" PC called out.

Silence.

The detective and the officer shared an uneasy look. Tran, hand on his holster, pushed further back into the shop.

"Hello?" PC called again. "Amanda? Joe?"

Nothing.

At the back of the shop, there was a door with an "Employees Only" sign. Tran nodded toward it.

Something metal crashed to the floor, followed closely by a yelp.

Tran drew his sidearm, and they both ran through the door. A figure pelted down the corridor.

"Stop!" Tran commanded.

The figure halted.

"Hands up!"

"W-wh-what's going on?" Amanda Watkins' voice trembled as she raised her arms.

"I'm so sorry. Ms. Watkins. We thought there was a robber or... something." Tran re-holstered his weapon.

"It's okay, but I have to get some paper towels." She hurried down the hall and returned with a fresh roll.

They followed her into a workroom and found a can of paint thinner on the floor next to a pool of clear liquid. The sharp smell of turpentine permeated the air. Amanda began peeling off paper towels and wadding them up to mop up the fluid.

"I kicked the can over when I stood up, and I didn't want it to damage the finish on the wood floors. Why on earth did you come back here waving a gun?" Annoyance was starting to displace fear in her voice.

"There was no one in the shop. I called out a few times, but nobody answered," PC used as calm a voice as she could muster. Adrenalin had flooded her system, too. "Then we heard the crash, and a scream. We were afraid you were getting robbed." *Or worse.*

Amanda pulled a trash bag from a drawer and started stuffing it with solvent-soaked paper towels. "What do you mean there was no one in the shop? Joe—" She cut herself off and sucked in a deep, angry breath. Her cheeks puffed as she let it out suddenly. "He was supposed to be at the register. He knew I was in the back, working on some new acquisitions."

The front door chime rang. Amanda glanced at the headphones on her desk. "When I'm listening to podcasts back here, I don't hear anything—noise canceling headphones." She frowned at the puckering clear coat on the oak floor. "Better see who that is."

She erupted through the Employees Only door, PC and Tran close behind. Joe Watkins sat on a stool behind the counter.

"Where have you been?" Amanda growled at her husband.

"Wow. You didn't need to call the police. I just went next door to drop off that package. Wanted to catch Drew before he left."

"First of all, I didn't call the police. Second, you could have left it in his mailbox at his house, if the gallery was closed."

Joe shrugged, unperturbed. "You were done with it. Thought I might as well be neighborly. I was only gone five minutes." He sulked. "So why are the cops here?"

"I just needed to clear up a couple of things. What package did you take to Drew?" PC asked, almost too boldly.

Amanda rolled her eyes. "It was an owl toothpick holder. Wing got broken off, and he wanted me to repair it. I don't know why he didn't just get one of the three we have left. It's not like they're expensive."

"Can I see them?"

"Of course."

"You said the three you have left. How many did you used to have?" PC followed Amanda to a glass case filled with knickknacks and china. A large plate with six irregular indentations forming a circle around a well in the center took pride of place in the heart of the display. Each indention was painted with a vibrantly colored sea-life scene.

"What kind of dish is that?"

Amanda followed her eyes. "It's a French oyster plate. I would love to have it at my house, but of course Joe is allergic to shellfish. I may take it home, anyway. Just because I have Oysters Rockefeller doesn't mean he has to. If you haven't had that at Truffles! you need to. Felix is a seafood maestro. Anyway, if you look to the left, you'll see the owls."

Sure enough, there amongst the junque, were three glass owl toothpick holders, all the same size and shape. One was white, like Drew's, but of the other two, one was blue and the other was pink.

"At one time we had five. They're really common, pretty easy to find at estate sales. Something like six months ago, Drew was in the shop and decided he liked them, so he got one. Then this guy came in and bought one Thursday morning."

"Do you remember his name?" PC was fairly sure she knew who it was.

"Let me look."

Amanda stalked back to the register and elbowed Joe out of the way. He almost spilled his microwave popcorn. She pulled a laptop from beneath the counter and opened the lid. *Tap tap tippity tap tap.*

"Looking at the sales receipts from Thursday, he paid with a Visa, and the name on the card was Peter S. Danvers."

"Can you print that?" Tran asked.

"Sure."

A printer behind the counter rattled to life and spat out a copy of Thursday's till. Amanda handed it to Tran.

"Thanks."

PC gave Amanda a friendly smile. "Could we step outside for a minute?"

The other two legs of Joe's stool hit the floor.

Amanda made a point of not looking at her husband. "Of course."

She led PC to the back door. "What is it?"

"You told us you got home at 8:30."

"So?" Amanda crossed her arms.

"Someone who was out walking a dog reported seeing a car pull up into your driveway at nine."

Amanda's head drooped, and she considered the floor. "I *did* get home at 8:30. But I found I was completely out of tempranillo. And chardonnay. So I went to Marberger's to buy more wine. I got back around nine."

"And you forgot to tell us?"

"Look, I didn't want the police chief to think I'm a lush. I'm sure there are plenty of other rumors floating around about me."

"I see. Thanks for clearing that up."

Amanda caressed the metal railing of the walkway. "If you're wondering where Joe was, he was in Horice, having a late dinner with someone. Probably Dinah Mae."

"I'm sorry."

"Yeah, well, I'm not sure if he wants to rub it in, or if he just doesn't care that I pay the credit card bills and I can see all the transactions." Amanda shook her head. "I really thought coming out here and running a business together would change things."

PC shifted her weight and looked at her FlitBit. This wasn't the kind of confession she'd been hoping for. "Have you considered counseling?" She couldn't think of anything else to say.

"The only thing that's keeping us together is that we sunk all of our money into the shop. We're comfortable, but not rich. On the off chance we could find a buyer for the store, the amount we could sell it for, divided by two, isn't enough for a fresh start. It's not exactly a secret around town that our marriage is mostly a business arrangement." Amanda shrugged. "You'd think he'd at least try to be discreet. But the joke's on his girlfriends. He can't afford to divorce me." She gave a bitter laugh.

Sounds like an episode of The First 48 *waiting to happen.* "I see." PC shifted her weight again. "I did have one other question. You said Joe was allergic to shellfish. What about you? Do you have any food allergies?"

"What? No." Amanda shook her head. "I don't understand."

"We found a piece of evidence that the killer might be severely allergic to something, and I think we'll find more evidence of that when the search continues at Mr. Burlesconi's house."

"Wait. Did you say 'killer?' I thought that man died of natural causes."

"There's reason to believe that he didn't, but the lab results will prove it one way or the other."

"That's just… I don't know what to say. Some stranger comes to Possumwood and gets himself murdered? That's like an Agatha Christie story or something."

Tran and PC left Vintage Glory and sat in the car, engine running.

"Where to now?" Tran asked.

"We should verify a few things in Horice. Let's start with Clovis Luxury Car. There's still have that big Academy store in town, right? I need to pick up a trail cam."

"Why a trail cam?"

"Because I've been spreading rumors that the killer probably left evidence at Drew's house, and the police are going to be searching for it. I want to make sure we see who shows up to reclaim it. I doubt that Woody—Chief Wilson—will authorize surveillance, especially since he thinks Drew is involved. I can't watch the place 24/7."

"Do you think he did it?"

"Do I think Drew killed Danvers? No. But he's also my friend, and I'm not sure I'm entirely impartial." PC looked out the passenger window. "Did you talk to Joe Watkins while I was outside with Amanda?"

"He did a lot of talking, but didn't really say much. He did admit that he was at the Big Red Brangus Steakhouse with Dinah Mae Brown after the meeting at Burlesconi's, though."

"That's one of the reasons we're going to Horice. Amanda had said as much. I need to see if there are any pictures of Joe from the shop's website, or the maybe the newspaper." She pulled out her smartphone.

She searched for the shop's website. She tapped the 'About Us' tab. There was a smiling Joe Watkins, standing next to an equally cheerful Amanda Watkins behind a chair that looked like it was from the 1500s. PC had a flash of Henry VIII, except with Joe's face, sitting there, waving a turkey leg and shouting, "Off with her head!" But that could have been based on the couple's animosity toward one another.

She opened another browser tab and found Dinah Mae's picture on the Mirabella County Historical Society's website.

The showroom at Clovis Luxury Car (Sales and Service with a Smile! according to the sign) was small, by car dealer standards, and displayed a single, mustard-yellow Maserati convertible. A man in a blue suit and a geometric print silk tie swept onto the floor, his laser-whitened smile dimming a bit when he saw a uniformed Tran.

"Welcome to Clovis Luxury Car. I'm Del. How can I help you find the car of your dreams?"

As his arm extended toward the convertible, PC noticed his suit cuffs were fraying, and he was missing a button from one sleeve. *Guess the luxury car market in the boondocks isn't exactly booming.*

PC smiled. "We're with the Possumwood Police Department. I think we're good on cars, but I would like to talk to your service manager."

Del moved behind the counter. "I would be delighted to schedule an appointment for you. What's the make and model of your car?"

"Oh, no thank you. I just need to verify that a customer was here on Thursday."

His high-wattage smile went slack, as the sales prospect, then service appointment slipped away. "I can help you with that, as well. Badge number, please?"

Tran showed his badge, and the salesman studied it for a few moments. He then looked to PC.

"She's a consultant for the department. I fully vouch for her."

Del hesitated, then began tapping on his hidden keyboard. "What day, did you say?"

PC answered. "It would have been Thursday evening. Don and Sofia Weingarten had their Mercedes towed here."

Del stopped typing and cocked his head to one side. "Yes. That was a strange pick up."

PC's ears pricked up. "Oh? How so?"

"The wrecker driver who was on call for us that night told me that a man had called requesting a tow in Possumwood, so he headed that way. After about fifteen minutes, a woman called and canceled. The driver had just gotten turned around and headed back to Horice when he got another Possumwood call, at a different address. He almost skipped it, because he thought he was being pranked. But he did go to the Weingartens' and collected their vehicle."

"Huh." PC sucked her teeth. "Do you know who the first caller was, or what kind of car?"

"No. Since it was canceled, the driver didn't keep a record."

"You've been very helpful, Mr....?"

"Clovis. Delbert Clovis. I'm the owner."

"Thank you, Mr. Clovis. We appreciate your help."

Back in the squad, Tran started the ignition and cranked up the AC. "So do think that canceled wrecker is related to the Danvers case, or just a weird coincidence?"

"Coincidences are like Bigfoot. They may exist, but there's no real proof. Do you know where the Big Red Brangus is, or do I need to get GPS?"

"I know where it is. It's about half a mile from here."

He pulled out of the parking space, and PC noticed his eyes linger on a red Ferrari. She smiled to herself. "Who do you think ordered the wrecker?"

Tran drummed his thumbs on the steering wheel. "It was a male. Danvers?"

"What about the female who canceled?"

"Good question."

PC adjusted her seatbelt. "If Danvers' car broke down, how did it get into Mirabella Lake?"

The light changed and Tran was able to pull onto the street. "I don't know. Maybe a woman came by and fixed it. Could have been something really minor, like a fuse."

"Why did she make the call instead of Danvers?"

Tran slowed to avoid a pothole. "Danvers was already dead?"

"So she threw him over her shoulder and carried him down the street to Drew's house?"

"Probably not."

"Well, Ada Dotson and the mayor saw somebody who could have been Danvers on his phone behind Vintage Glory. Maybe he was talking to the wrecker driver, and encountered the killer after he hung up. Could have even been Ada and Phineas that lured him into the alley behind Drew's house and gave him the injection." PC raised her hands, frustrated.

"I find that hard to believe. Why would they want to kill him?"

"I'm just throwing stuff at the wall to see if anything sticks. I don't know how much you've read of the reports, but did you know that the mayor doesn't seem to have existed before 1997?"

"I did *not* know that." Tran made a right turn.

"I'd like to talk to him after we finish up here, if it's not too late. Maybe he was raised by wolves, and they failed to apply for his Social Security card. Or maybe he changed his identity. If that's so, could be he's the one the IRS is after, for something he did in a previous life."

Tran was silent as he drove the last few blocks to the steakhouse. There were no cars in the parking lot, but it was too early for dinner and awfully late for lunch. PC pushed open the faux weathered door, and they stepped into the cool dimness.

"Table for two?" The hostess, dressed in black, pulled two menus from the bin.

"Actually," PC said, "we're here on official business. Possumwood PD. Is there anyone working tonight in the front of the house who was also working on Thursday?"

"I was."

"Excellent." PC pulled out her phone and woke it. The picture of Joe Watkins smiled back at her. She showed it to the young woman. "Do you recognize this man?"

"Sure. That's Mr. Watkins. He comes in at least every other Thursday. Always requests table twelve." She gestured to a table tucked away in the corner furthest from the front door.

"Great." PC tapped her phone. "What about her?"

The hostess looked at Dinah Mae's photo. "Yeah. I think that was the lady who was here with him. He, um, dates a lot of women."

Of course he does. "Thanks for your time." PC read the nametag on the hostess' dress. "Jennifer. If you don't mind, I need your last name for my notes."

"Oh. Sure. Morales."

"And also an address and phone number."

Jennifer told her, and PC snapped her notebook closed.

"Got it. Thanks."

When they got back to the car, she got out her notebook and scribbled in it for a few minutes.

"You know, your phone has a voice recorder."

"I'm aware of that, Tran." PC wrote some more.

"Well, wouldn't it be faster to just record that stuff and transcribe it later? You can get software to do that."

"Writing it down helps me remember." She snapped the book closed. "Let's get to Academy. I think we'll have to chat with the mayor in the morning."

PC left Tran to browse the exercise equipment of the sporting goods store while she headed to the hunting section for a trail camera. It was more expensive than she wanted, but she chose one with wi-fi and cloud back up. She could set it to alert on her phone whenever it detected movement.

Tran dropped her at the station. She drove to Drew's to set up the camera.

She knocked. Moments later, the front door swung open. "Hey, PC."

She stepped inside, compact game camera, still in its Academy bag, tucked under her arm. "I just wanted to come by and talk to you for a little bit. There's been a development in the Danvers case."

"Oh?" Drew's eyebrows arched. "Why don't we sit down?"

"Yes. Before we get into that, I'm curious about something. I know you were interviewed, but I haven't seen the transcript. What did you do on Thursday night after the meeting?"

He led the way to the kitchen and pulled out a stool from the breakfast bar. PC set the camera on the countertop before she pulled out her own stool and perched on it.

"Can I get you anything to drink?"

"Just water."

He went to the cupboard and got two glasses.

"After everyone left, I cleaned up the dishes. I was out of flour and eggs, and a few other things, so I thought I'd make a quick grocery run before they closed. I went to Marberger's."

"Did you happen to see Amanda Watkins there?"

He filled the glasses with chilled water from the fridge. "I did, actually. She was just leaving as I was coming in from the parking lot. We said 'Hello,' but nothing more than that."

PC nodded. He set the two glasses on the bar and slid onto his own stool. His eyes rested momentarily on the bag. "After I started the car, my low fuel light came on, so I got gas at the truck stop. Got a car wash, too. They were shutting down as I went through—I didn't get a chance to vacuum. Then I came home."

"What time did you arrive?"

"Not really sure. Car wash closes at ten, so probably 10:15 ish."

If Drew is the killer, he could have dispatched Danvers at any time after the meeting. If not, there's an hour and a half window where he wasn't home, and anyone could have done it.

PC re-adjusted her seat on the stool. "Some new evidence turned up. There's a possibility that Danvers didn't die of natural causes."

"What? I thought the coroner said it was an aneurysm."

He looks surprised, but not anxious. "They won't know for sure until the labs come back. The aneurysm may be the cause of death, but it may not be the manner." *Should I ask him?* "Do you, by chance, have any food allergies?"

"MSG gives me horrible headaches and bloating. Also, I can't touch sesame seeds."

"But you wouldn't die from it."

"What's this about?"

"We have reason to believe that the killer might have a food allergy."

Drew took a sip of his water. "I'm not sure if I should be hurt that you think I might have done this, or admire your rigorous detective work."

His face was blank, unreadable. PC had a choice to make, and there was a high price for picking wrong.

"There's a rumor going around town that police will be looking for some specific evidence at your house."

He crossed his arms and leaned back a little. "I wonder how that got started."

PC pulled the trail cam out of its bag. "I was hoping that the killer would show up to look for the evidence that they thought they'd disposed of, and I wanted to catch them in the act."

Drew blinked a few times, then a smile cracked his lips. He finally gave in and chuckled. "That's so crazy, it might just work. Where do you want to set it up?"

They went out to the courtyard to scout a location. Drew tried the camera in different places, and PC used the video link on her phone to check the view. They found a spot on one of the oak trees where the camera was mostly hidden by an azalea bush, but it still got a good shot of anyone near the toolshed.

"Will you call me if you spot anyone creeping around in my courtyard?"

"Of course."

His eyes softened. "You going to be at darts tomorrow?"

PC tucked her phone into her bag. "Wouldn't miss it. But now, I've got to go feed. You can probably hear Mama's donkeys braying from here, if meals are late."

He held her eyes just a moment too long. She looked away and turned toward the door. Drew walked her to the front porch.

"See you tomorrow." He gave her the vaguest of waves.

"Night."

PC could have lingered there, chatting in the parlor. Probably best not to, not tonight, anyway. She walked to her car and got in. She noticed Drew standing on the porch, watching her. Was it to make sure that she got on her way safely, or something else? Once the engine started, he went inside.

Had she made the right choice to enlist his help with the camera? Even if he was the killer, he had every legitimate reason for being out in his own yard, so that would prove nothing. If the real killer showed up, it was better he knew what was happening, so he didn't go out and confront them. In retrospect, she probably should have asked him first before she used his courtyard to bait a trap. But sometimes it's better to beg forgiveness than permission.

She'd talked to killers on an almost daily basis for the last twenty-five years. Drew checked none of the boxes on the guilty murderer checklist. And if she'd used a pretext to make Drew go inside, then hidden the camera, he'd probably never speak to her again after he found it.

No, she did the right thing. Probably.

Chapter 15

PC NEEDED AN extra-large cup of coffee. The camera had sent her notification at 10:42 and a photo of a bat fluttering around the courtyard. At 12:31, it woke her when a raccoon had noticed something shiny and come to investigate. A mother opossum, loaded down with eight babies, lumbered by at 2:12. An early rising cottontail rabbit checked in at 4:20. All cute. No killer. She forwarded the photos to Drew while she was waiting on coffee to brew.

What went wrong? Had her story not had time to spread to the killer? Did the killer sidestep the trap? Was Drew the killer? PC shook her head. She'd leave the trail cam up again tonight, in case she'd overestimated the speed of small town gossip. She could help that along when she and Tran went to visit Mayor Scott.

PC ran through her morning chores as quickly as she could and showered before she headed for the station. Tran was waiting for her in the lobby.

"You ready to see the mayor?"

"Ready as I'm likely to get." An exhausted PC felt like she was wading through molasses after her nocturnal wildlife theater experience.

They walked across the street to City Hall, and Tran led the way up the well-worn stairs to the mayor's office. A wooden door, about a third of which was frosted glass, bore the word 'MAYOR' in a dark gold Art Deco font. PC turned the knob, and they both found themselves in the reception area of Phineas Scott's office.

A woman, close to retirement age, PC guessed, looked up at them through owlish, upside-down frame glasses, the kind that had been popular in the 80s.

Her words may have said, "May I help you?" but her tone said, "Go away."

PC gave a practiced smile. "Is Mayor Scott available? It's Tran and Donovan from the police."

The woman's eyes rested on Tran. "I can see that. I'll let him know you're here."

She punched a button on the phone and waited a second. "Possumwood PD is here for you." She didn't wait for a response before hanging up.

A few seconds later, Phineas Scott appeared in the doorway to the left of the receptionist's desk.

"Detective Donovan, Officer Tran. Come in, come in!"

PC thought he was oddly cheerful as he ushered them into his office, gesturing for them to sit in upholstered chairs in front of his desk.

A dark shape moved in the corner and PC's breath caught in her throat. Then she realized that it was just Scott's dog, Anubis, sitting up on his bed and stretching.

"How can I help Possumwood's finest this morning?"

"Well," PC leaned forward in her chair. "There's been a development in the Danvers case, and I wanted to clarify some things with you."

Scott's shoulders visibly relaxed, and he leaned back in his leather executive chair. "Excellent. What's the news?"

"Special Agent Danvers' car was found in Mirabella Lake. I'm sure you knew that. But we found some evidence that the killer might have had a severe food allergy."

"Wait-wait-wait. Did you say killer?"

"Yes. Dr. Mack won't know for sure until all the labs come back, but there is reasonable suspicion that it was a murder. In fact, we're going back to Mr. Burlesconi's home later to search for an additional piece of evidence."

Scott sat up. "What kind of evidence?"

Tran cleared his throat. "We can't really go into that, sir. It is an ongoing investigation."

The mayor's head bobbed like a fishing float when minnows are stealing the bait. "Of course. Thanks for stopping by to keep me informed." He stood up as if to dismiss them.

Tran and PC remained seated.

"Actually," PC pulled her notebook from her bag. "There's something else we need to clear up."

"Oh?" Scott turned paler as he sat mechanically in his seat. Anubis growled.

"It's alright, Nubie. It's okay. Don't fuss."

The dog quieted.

"So I was doing some standard background check information, and I found some interesting things about you."

By this time, Scott's face had taken on a greenish tinge, and PC wondered if he was going to vomit. She glanced around for a trash can, but didn't see one.

"And what were those things?" His pupils closed in and a bead of sweat popped up on his forehead.

"When I was looking at your documents, it seems that no such person as Phineas Scott existed before 1997."

The mayor dropped his head, rubbing the bridge of his nose with his left hand. "I was afraid of this."

How afraid? Afraid enough to kill? PC felt her pulse quicken. "Would you care to elaborate?"

Scott turned his chair toward the window and stood up. He strode over to the glass and stood there with his back to them. PC's eyes scanned the casing, trying to determine if the window could be opened. Then he turned to face them and sat on the wide windowsill.

"I think, actually, it'll be a relief to talk about it. Secrets just weigh you down, don't they? Kinda like filling your pockets with rocks and wading out into the ocean." He smiled ruefully and returned to his chair. Then he leaned forward and spoke softly. "I know I don't really have a good excuse. I did what I did. It seemed like the right thing to do back then. If I could go back in time, I would never have done it." He went silent.

"Are you saying you killed Danvers?" Tran asked.

PC wanted to smack him. She'd have to give him some training on interrogating suspects later. When they're talking, shut up and let them talk.

Scott's head jerked up. "What? No! That's not at all what I'm saying. I'm in the witness protection program." He shook his head. "Coming out of college, I owed too much money. I could pay rent and my loans, but not keep the lights on and eat. So I did some courier work."

"Like a bicycle messenger?" Tran asked.

"I wish. I delivered packages for a man who called himself Demonio. He had gang tattoos, so I assumed it was drugs, but I didn't ask and I didn't look inside. I made $100 cash for every delivery. On top of my day job, I worked four nights a week and made usually four or five deliveries a night. Got a nice apartment, new car. I had just paid off my student loans, and I was starting to think about easing out of the mule business.

"I'd made the last run of the night and was getting back in my car when two guys grabbed me from behind and put a cloth bag over my head. I just knew they were going to kill me. They shoved me into the back seat of a car and we started driving.

"Eventually, the car stopped, and a man spoke to me.

"We know what you've been up to, Jeffrey—that used to be my name. You just delivered a kilo of cocaine to a police officer, and we have it on film."

"Long story short, I testified against some members of a drug cartel, and the state gave me a new identity and home. I don't know how closely you've read the historical marker in the park." He leaned his head toward the window. "But the founder of the town was Zachariah Phineas Prescott Justice."

PC tamped down a smile. "Phineas Scott, man in the middle."

Scott relaxed back into his chair. "Exactly. So what happens now?"

She looked at Tran, then back to the mayor. "Nothing."

"Nothing?"

"Nothing. Your situation's confidential. But I am curious. Running for political office seems pretty risky, if you're in the witness protection program. Why did you do it?"

"Well, Demonio's dead, along with most of his crew. I think one or two are either on death row or serving life in prison. Nobody cares about a snitch from twenty plus years ago."

Claws clicked on the hardwood floor as Anubis stalked over from his bed to sit next to his master. PC could feel his yellow eyes disapproving of her, even though she couldn't see them.

She stood up, and Tran did the same. "Thank you, Mayor Scott. I appreciate you clearing things up for me." She leaned in toward him. "And I have never, ever burned a confidential informant."

His smile was weak as ketchup soup. "Thank you."

When they got back, video from the ranger station at Mirabella Creek SP had arrived. Tran downloaded it from the cloud and they watched it on a computer monitor. At 1:00 AM Friday morning, someone parked a car with the driver's door just out of range of the camera. They got out of the car and came around the passenger side, wearing a baseball cap with a hoodie pulled over the top of it, and baggy pants. The person manually opened the gate, got back in the car the same way they'd left it, and drove the car through. They got out and closed the gate, then continued down the park road. They fast-forwarded through the video until daylight, but the hooded figure never reappeared.

Tran had to leave for an appointment, and PC spent the rest of the afternoon going over reports and looking at the physical evidence in the case. By the end of the day, she didn't feel like she was a millimeter closer to solving the case than she had been on Saturday. If you just can't make the pieces fit, sometimes the best thing to do is something else.

She'd push the case to the back of her mind and let it percolate, a strategy that had worked for her so many times before. She cleaned up the papers spread across the conference table and left to feed the animals before going to darts.

Nothing like a nice, relaxing game of darts with friends. And maybe a killer.

Chapter 16

PC WAS GLAD that she'd walked to the Biersal. There wasn't a parking spot to be had, and that was unusual for a Wednesday night.

What is going on?

She entered through the back door, as per usual, and found the place heaving with people. People standing around with little plastic plates filled with hors d'oeuvres. People holding plastic glasses of beer and wine. A booth by the door carried a large sign: Drink and Food Tickets.

When she looked toward the dart boards, they were covered with a banner that read, "Mirabella County Historical Society" on one line and "Annual Benefit" on the next.

PC sighed and maneuvered herself out of the way of traffic, against the wall. She'd never find Drew in this sea of people, so she texted him.

"You at Biersal?"

"Yes. Forgot it was benefit night. In line for drink—want anything?"

"Sure, as long as it isn't persimmon ale."

"LOL. Where are you?"

"Wall between back door and restrooms."

"Got it. See you soon. Maybe."

PC hated big crowds. They depleted her energy and made her feel queasy. With all due respect to the Historical Society, she wanted nothing more than to get her drink and get out of there. The Biersal did have a biergarten on the other side of the building—with any luck, it was less crowded there. She couldn't really check it out until Drew found her, but she could hope.

He turned up almost ten minutes later, holding a cup of beer in one hand and a glass of wine in the other. "You have a preference?"

PC noticed a smudge that looked suspiciously like a lip print on the edge of the beer glass. "The one you haven't drunk out of."

"Sorry. Force of habit." He handed her the wine.

She gave the plastic cup a swirl. "This is very dark wine." It reminded her of the color of clotted blood. Gingerly, she took a sip. "What kind is it?"

"You don't like it?"

"It's… different. I'm not a connoisseur—if you blindfolded me, I probably couldn't tell merlot from chardonnay, but this doesn't taste quite like anything I've ever had."

"Is that good?" Drew sipped his beer.

"I'll let you know." She tried another taste of the wine. "Do you want to—"

A throaty scream cut her off.

All heads turned to the front door. Victoria Deen came running in, swinging her clutch purse wildly. "Why?" she yelled. "It's almost dark. Why are there bees?"

Flustered, she tried to compose herself at the bar with a glass of water. The hum of many conversations resumed, a white noise that made PC feel itchy.

"As I was saying. You want to see if the biergarten is less crowded?"

"Sure."

They threaded their way through the throng, and had to pass just behind the drink station that had been set up between pool tables, which had been swaddled in plastic and held a variety of finger foods. But it was the bottles of wine that caught her eye.

Sagrantino. The same type that Peter Danvers had bought a case of before he died, but was not in his hotel room nor in his car. Had the killer brought it? Good way to dispose of it.

"Excuse me," she tapped on the side of the table.

"I'm sorry, the end of the line is over there." The bartender gestured to the people standing in front of him.

"I know that. Where did this wine come from?"

"I don't know. It was here when I got here. Next, please. Your drink ticket?"

PC left him dealing with a tall man and his much shorter companion.

"C'mon." She tugged at Drew's sleeve.

"I thought we were going outside."

"In a minute. I have to check something out first."

She'd caught a glimpse of Stan Zimmerman, one of the owners, behind the bar. He was at the opposite end, slicing fruit. It took her a few tries to get his attention, but he finally came over.

"Is there something I can help you with?" he asked.

"Yes, actually. I was really curious about this wine. It's very unusual. Do you know where it came from?"

"No idea. We provided the beer and the venue. The Historical Society provided everything else."

"Thanks."

Stan turned back to what he had been doing. PC looked around. Was Dinah Mae here? Would she know how it got here? Did she bring it?

The squeal of feedback from a microphone made PC cringe. There was a small stage area on the side of the bar closest to the front door, and Mayor Scott stood on it.

He tapped the mic. "Is this thing on?"

Don't quit your day job.

The Mayor grinned. "On behalf of the Mirabella County Historical society, I'd like to thank everyone for coming out tonight. Don't forget to visit the biergarten and make a bid on the silent auction items that many of our county-wide business owners have donated. Thank you. Enjoy your evening."

Mirabella County had a population of about thirty thousand, and it seemed to PC that every one of them, and half of their friends, were at the Biersal. Even with the big ceiling fans on, the air seemed close, stifling.

PC pulled the front of her shirt a few times to generate a micro-breeze. "Let's have a look in the biergarten."

Drew dropped his empty glass in the recycling bin. "Planning on making a bid?"

"I mostly need some air."

Drew forged ahead, plowing his way through the crowd to the side door. Outside, the evening air was verging on cool, and PC felt she could breathe again. A couple dozen people milled around the folding tables that held the various offerings by local businesses.

"Good evenin', Drew." Dinah Mae Brown cooed. "And Detective Donovan."

The tilt of her head and the arch of her eyebrow made PC wonder what conclusions she was jumping to.

Dinah Mae handed each of them a brochure printed on standard copy paper and folded in thirds. "Not all the silent auction items are on display. Bids will be accepted until the thirty-first, then the winners will be announced at the Battle of Mirabella Creek re-enactment next month. Photos and more in-depth descriptions are on our website."

The tables were arranged in a C shape that opened toward the side door, and a pop-up awning sheltered each table. A high-intensity camping lantern, suspended from the center, lighted each awning. Amanda Watkins stood by one table, talking to a young couple. Whether she was promoting the shop's donation or keeping an eye on Dinah Mae, PC couldn't guess—none of the other tables were manned. Perhaps it was both. PC and Drew nodded to her as they passed, not wanting to interrupt her conversation.

PC stopped in front of an 11 x 17 framed canvas, depicting an impressionist style painting of Texas bluebonnets and Indian paintbrushes on a hill at sunset. Or sunrise. "I didn't know your gallery participated in the auction."

Drew smiled. "Of course. Every year. Wilma Gatewood painted this—you took one of her acrylics workshops a couple of weeks ago. She'd been to that Impressionist exhibit at the Museum of Fine Arts in Houston, so she tried out some of their techniques."

PC remembered seeing the announcement in the MFA newsletter months ago. She'd wanted to go, but hadn't found the time.

Drew continued. "Wilma prefers acrylics, but she did this one is in oils, because she thought she could get a closer match to the style of the Garden at Giverny. Did you know that was actually Monet's back yard, and also where he painted his waterlilies series? Most people think it's a single painting, but there are around two hundred fifty canvases, painted over twenty years." He stopped talking and looked at the table. "I'm giving you another TED Talk, aren't I?"

"I like that you seem to know something about almost everything." She winked at him. "Saves me from having to go to Wikipedia."

PC really did like the painting. She didn't expect to win, but she planned to put in a bid on it—it would be perfect for that bare spot behind the recliner in her Houston house. But she didn't want to right here, right now, with Drew standing over her shoulder. If she didn't win, she could always ask Wilma about how to do that style at the next workshop, and paint one for herself.

One of the items on offer was six months of service from End Results, a company that offered pet waste scooping and disposal. PC made a mental note to call them about scooping up after Rose's animals once PC went back to Houston. Of course, it would be a lot cheaper to get Rocky to do it, but she wasn't entirely convinced that his newfound responsible phase was going to last. He'd had a job for three months now, and hadn't bolted, but his record was five months, so there was still time. Then she felt bad for not giving him the benefit of the doubt.

She drained the last of her wine, deciding that she liked it after all. But now she needed a trip to the ladies' room.

They finished the circuit of auction items. They'd ranged from the silly—a box of Possumwood soil—to the sublime: an intricate stained-glass window, depicting a double-flowering hibiscus with a hummingbird hovering in front of it, ready to take a sip of nectar.

"I'm ready to go back inside—I need to make a pit stop."

"Sure. Let me dispose of this for you." Drew took the plastic cup from her hand.

Back inside, it felt more crowded than ever. PC made her way to the restrooms. Thankfully, the line wasn't horrendously long. She'd just closed the stall door when she heard two women come in.

"Okay, can you bend over a little bit? I can't believe you got a bracelet caught in your hair."

Was that Ada Dotson?

"Uggh! I love this Faberge, but it gets caught on *everything*."

Who was that? Could it be Sylvia Marberger?

"Okay. I'm doing the best I can."

"Ow!"

"Sorry."

PC took care of business as fast as she could, hoping to come out before the two ladies finished and left.

"There. It's out."

"Thanks."

PC opened the door to find Ada Dotson washing her hands. Victoria Deen was repairing her messy bun in the mirror.

Victoria's eyes narrowed when she saw PC, and she strode out of the room without a word, a bejeweled filigree pendant just above her cleavage, and oblong charms on her pale wrist sparkling under the pulsing fluorescent light.

"Hey, Ada."

Her grey hair was braided and coiled into a severe bun, but a few tendrils had escaped to curl around her face. Cloisonne earrings in peacock shades dangled from her ears. PC thought she looked very elegant, out of place at a beer hall fundraiser.

"PC. I didn't expect to see you here."

The detective moved to the sink and turned on the water. "I didn't expect to be here."

The soap was thin and slimy, and she couldn't help showing her disgust.

Ada's lips tighten. "Yes. That's what I thought, too. Someone should tell those Zimmerman boys that Justice Johnson sells wonderful goat-milk soap."

"I agree. But at least there's excellent wine, though, right? Did you supply that?"

"Sure did." Ada fluffed her hair in the mirror. "Two cases each of chardonnay and cabernet."

"Oh? I had a glass of Sagrantino. Which was strange, because I'd never even heard of it, until you mentioned it the other day. But it was good wine, though."

Ada shrugged. "Well, someone provided it, but it wasn't me. I can order a case for you, if you want—just stop by the store. See you later."

She left while PC looked forlornly at the empty paper towel dispenser and overflowing trash bin. With nothing else to do, she wiped her wet hands on her pants and went to find Drew.

He hadn't strayed far from the bathroom area and stood talking to Don and Sofia Weingarten, close to the back side of the bar. PC got a glass of water before she joined the small group.

"Well, good evening, Detective." Don Weingarten's voice was as slimy as the soap. "How's your not-a-murder case going?"

"You might be surprised at the sorts of things I've found out. There are a number of people who might have wanted Mr. Danvers dead."

Sofia sucked in a sharp breath. "Are you saying there may be a killer on the loose?"

"Possibly. I don't know if your husband told you we found some evidence that it might not be natural causes."

PC could have tried to allay her fears by telling her that unless she was involved in serious tax crimes, she wasn't likely in any danger. Pete Danvers was almost certainly not a random victim. But she didn't. If the Weingartens were involved, she wanted them to sweat. And maybe come to Drew's house to search the courtyard for evidence in the middle of the night. The trail cam was still up.

Don squeezed his wife's shoulder. "She said it *might* be a murder, so just calm down. It probably isn't. I'll wager it's some kinky sex thing that went horribly wrong."

Drew cleared his throat.

"Sorry," Don backtracked. "I didn't mean to imply…"

"Of course, you didn't." Drew's voice dripped sarcasm.

"Well." Don clasped his wife's hand. "Poor Sofia has been on her feet all day long helping get the place set up for tonight. I'm going to take her home to relax."

PC smiled at Sofia. "How many people does it take to set up a big event like this?"

"There were a number of us, but I didn't really count."

Don's grip on her hand tightened and Sofia winced.

The detective restrained herself from scolding him. "Not that I'm planning any events or anything. I was just curious. I'm sure Dinah Mae was here supervising."

"She and Amanda were here all day. Had some brawny young men setting up tables and chairs. Ada was here for a while—she had those same guys bring in the wine." Sofia gave a little laugh. "The mayor came by to do a mic check. Even Victoria Deen was here for a little bit."

PC wanted to ask more questions, but Don cut in.

"We really have to be going."

PC watched him practically drag her out the door.

"Well. That was… interesting."

"Yeah. Don can be a jerk, but he's not all bad. I wouldn't want to be Sofia, though."

PC shot-gunned the rest of her water. When she turned to take the real glass tumbler back to the bar, she nearly crashed into Joe Watkins.

"I am so sorry!"

"Don't worry about it. Cliff and I were just about to go for a smoke outside." He looked toward the back door. PC recognized Clifton Goodnight as the next-door neighbor of the Biersal who had recently caused some trouble for the owners of Happily Ever Afters across the street. But the neighborhood feud had since been resolved.

"Hey, Cliff."

"Hey." He raised an unlit cigar. PC wasn't sure if it was meant as a salute, or a gesture of impatience.

The two men wove between clumps of people and made their way out the door. PC was also ready to bolt for the exit. Being in a big crowd like this was just exhausting.

She turned to Drew. "Thanks for the wine, but I really should go."

"I wasn't planning to stay much longer, either."

Somewhere to PC's right came a distinctive *pltttt* of a fart. It was loud enough that Drew's head turned in that direction, too. Within seconds, a noxious odor drifted over them.

Yuck. That smells just like when Cordite rolled in rotten eggs.

"Let's make a break for the parking lot, shall we?" Drew took her elbow.

They were almost to the door when PC stopped. "I know who the killer is."

Chapter 17

"WHAT?" DREW ASKED. "Who is it?"

"I'll explain later!" PC called over her shoulder as she started to jog down the street to Rose's house. She would call Tran as soon as she got there, and they would come up with a plan.

It was warm enough that PC was drenched in sweat when she arrived and had to take a little time to catch her breath. When she stopped panting, she got out her phone.

Tran didn't answer.

Where is he?

She sent him a text: "I know who killed Pete Danvers,"

Ten minutes later, he still hadn't replied.

He's probably out with Annie. Good for him, bad for me.

Reluctantly, she texted Woody: "Can you meet me at the station? I know who killed Danvers."

He replied almost instantly. "Already there"

PC grabbed her bag and car keys. Rocky and Cordite were lounging on the couch, eating potato chips, when she went through the living room.

PC frowned at her brother. "I wish you wouldn't feed him junk food. He's getting to be a little chunky monkey."

"But he loves it! What's the point of living, if you can't enjoy treats sometimes?"

She rolled her eyes. "Listen, I have to go out for a little while. Can you take Cordie out to pee when your show's over?"

"I hope you're not going on a date looking like that."

"Work."

She left before he could say anything else. When she arrived at the cop shop, Woody was leaning on the front desk, chatting with the officer who'd drawn the dispatch duty short straw.

"It's about time you got here, Donovan."

"You ready to catch a killer?"

Thursday Night Live, as put on by the Justice Avenue Baptist, had shifted venues, going from the Azalea Manor nursing home to its own building. Victoria Deen had taken the service over, and she just didn't have the come-to-Jesus revival tent vibe that her husband had. A former cheerleader, music and dancing were more in her wheelhouse. She arranged for musical groups, with or without dancers, one-act players, and Christian stand-up comedians. This played to a very different audience than its former iteration. While it may not have been SRO, it was definitely popular, and even people who didn't attend Justice Baptist came for the shows.

The gospel group had already taken the stage when PC slipped into a seat in the back row. Out of about 500 seats, more than half were filled, mostly the ones closest to the stage. She looked around, trying to pick out familiar faces. She thought she saw the Weingartens sitting in the center section, third row from the front. And perhaps Ada Dotson was in the left wing, almost as far back as PC. There was a vibrant light show throbbing along with the music, and it was a little hard to tell.

Three women in sequined dresses stood at the front of the stage, while a choir of ten sang backing vocals and provided hand gestures with a few minimal dance moves. PC didn't know most of the songs, but the group was better than she expected, and she found her head bobbing to the faster songs. The detective buttoned her light sweater—the AC was cranked to eleven.

The evening's entertainment was scheduled to take an hour, then they played a ten-minute encore. She stared at the half-page printed program in her hands, and it made her feel not so much sad as resigned. The show finished and Victoria had her assistant pastor give the benediction while she hurried up the aisle in her white stilettos to mingle with the flock as they exited. Worshippers streamed out, loop currents forming around islands of people who'd stopped to catch up on the latest gossip.

PC waited.

As the last group drifted to the door, PC spoke softly into the empty space.

"It's go time."

"I'm at the front," Woody's voice sounded in her ear. "Tran and Sanchez are at the back door."

Victoria Deen was talking to an older couple. Her nostrils flared and her jaw clenched when she saw PC standing by the door. Once the couple turned toward the exit, she stalked over to the detective, heels clicking angrily on the granite-tiled lobby floor.

"You have some nerve coming here," Victoria snarled.

PC shrugged. "You have some nerve claiming to be a spiritual leader."

Victoria's face darkened "What is that supposed to mean?"

"Why was the IRS surveilling you? Money laundering? Tax evasion? Embezzlement?"

"I don't know what you're talking about."

"Oh, Vicky. I wish that were true. Shall I tell you a story?"

Victoria crossed her arms. "Could I stop you?"

"No." PC shifted just a little to correct the aim of the camera that was hidden in her pendant. "But you can fill in the details. Once upon a time, there was a preacher's wife. She wasn't a big fan of ministering to the sick, but she did like all of that collection plate cash. And lucky for her, she was the one who counted the money and entered it in the ledger. The CPA never even knew that what bountifully flowed in and what showed up in the books were two different numbers. But somewhere, she made a mistake, and the IRS decided to investigate. Maybe she figured it out, or maybe he contacted her, but she learned the new guy hanging around town, Pete Danvers, was an IRS Special Agent."

Victoria's head shook like a bobble head in an earthquake. Her eyes flashed with anger, and PC remained wary, because the preacher's wife looked like she might leap on her like a starving tiger at any moment.

"At some point, this sticky-fingered lady made her way to the agent's hotel room and noticed that he took heart medication. Because she was severely allergic to bees, she carried an epinephrine injector with her at all times. And being a good patient, she'd read every last warning label. She knew that a shot of it could kill someone with heart trouble, so she made a plan."

"This should be good," Victoria snarled.

PC ignored her. "Last Thursday, after the Thursday Night Live program finished, either she called Agent Danvers and asked him to meet, or she just happened to see his car parked at Vintage Glory. Either way, she was driving, because hiking for a few generously sized city blocks in five-inch heels is no fun."

"She sounds very clever."

"Now people might see her flashy white BMW parked downtown and wonder what was going on, so she pretended to be broken down. She pulled one of the fuses, just in case anyone got too helpful and tried to start the car. Her plan almost fell apart when white knight Tim Kowalski came riding to the rescue and called a tow truck for her. But she ditched Tim and canceled the wrecker."

"You should write a book or something. You have a vivid imagination."

"Either that, or I worked homicide for twenty-five years." PC smiled like a shark catching the scent of blood. "Anyway. This clever girl made contact with Agent Danvers and got in his car. That's when she accidentally dropped the fuse by his car in the parking spot. But no problem—they usually come in a multi-pack, and there's probably more in her car."

Victoria grunted, but she shifted her weight away from PC.

"For whatever reason, Danvers parked in the maintenance alley that runs behind the Burlesconi house. And that's where she lured him into the toolshed, perhaps with the promise of a little hanky-panky. Once inside, she jabbed him in the neck with her injector. He tried to dodge it, but got scratched by the needle. She took the pen away with her, but the cap had rolled under the seat of his car when she prepared it earlier.

"I don't know if she waited for him to lose consciousness before she left him there to die. At some point before she covered him up, she noticed that he held one of the programs from the church service clenched in his fist, and when she ripped it away, it must have been balled up enough that she didn't notice that the top left corner where it says 'Justice Avenue Baptist Church' was torn, and the Justice part stayed with Agent Danvers." PC held up her copy of the current schedule.

"After that, she drove his car to her house and parked it in the garage. She slipped into something more comfortable and waited until she thought traffic had died down enough, then she went to Agent Danvers' motel room, and let herself in with his key to gather up all of his belongings, especially his computer. She drove to Mirabella Creek Park, opened the gate, then rolled down all the windows so she wouldn't get trapped, and drove down the boat ramp until the car engine became submerged and cut out. The rest was easy—she walked the two miles back home, changed back into her Thursday Night Live clothes, replaced the fuse, and drove her own car home."

"Are you done with your fantasy story? Because it sounds like you don't have any actual evidence to charge her."

"That's where you're wrong. Do you remember getting your bracelet caught in your hair last night at the Biersal?"

Victoria's eyes narrowed. "I don't see what that has to do with anything."

"You said 'I love this Faberge, but it catches on everything.' Later, when somebody made an egregious fart, it hit me like a ton of rotten eggs. Faberge is famous for eggs. And that really fancy bead I found in Danvers' motel room is from your egg charm bracelet. It must have caught on something while you were ransacking the place. If you look at your wrist, you can see there's a gap where a charm is missing."

Victoria's face contorted, her jaw clenching over and over. She took a deep breath, as if she were about to spring into either fight or flight.

PC had to catch her off guard. "I do have one question, though. The night Heather Micah was murdered at the Azalea Manor, you weren't there. Where were you?"

Victoria laughed bitterly. "Heather Micah. She bled Josh for years until he told her he was broke. I guess she believed him, because she left him alone, at least for a little while. When she blew into town, I knew there was only one reason she'd come back here. But I beat her to the punch. That Thursday, I was wiring money to my Caymans bank account, where neither she, nor the IRS could get at it." She tossed her head, an ugly smirk crinkling her mouth.

"Did you get that?" PC asked.

"Get what?" Victoria's face went slack as the answer dawned on her. "You're wearing a wire, aren't you?"

"Yes. And the police are at both doors to the sanctuary."

The front door opened and Woody stepped inside. PC could tell that the preacher's wife was running a cost benefit analysis on an escape attempt.

Victoria gazed up at the out-sized stained-glass mural that spread across the front of the building, then sighed.

She'd made her decision.

The sharp tapping of Victoria's heels echoed through the empty chamber as she strode across the granite floor toward Woody.

"Good evening, Chief. I'd like to talk to my lawyer."

Chapter 18

FRIDAY AFTERNOON, THE whole town was abuzz. Annie even let it slip to PC that a one-way ticket to Andorra was found in Victoria's purse, along with her passport. She had just finished offshoring all her money and was headed to the airport Friday morning. The IRS had swept in to raid the Justice Street Baptist Church. PC wondered if Supervisory Special Agent Newman was there, so she stopped by to see.

An agent stopped her from entering the building. "I'm sorry. They're executing a search warrant. You'll have to leave."

"I just wondered if SSA Newman was here. I would like to speak with her."

"I'm sorry. You'll have to leave."

"I wanted to ask about Agent Faudi. Last I heard, she was in critical condition, but I don't know how she's doing. She got hurt out here…"

The agent was silent for several long moments.

"What's your name?"

"PC Donovan."

The agent turned his head and spoke into the radio on his shoulder. "Bragg, could you ask the SSA if she wants to talk to a PC Donovan?"

A few minutes later, Newman walked through the door.

"Detective Donovan. How are you?" If her smile wasn't genuine, it was an excellent forgery.

"Good. How is Agent Faudi?"

"She came out of the coma yesterday. She'll survive. Everything else remains to be seen."

"Well, that's progress, right?"

"Yes. I suppose it is."

"Do you mind my asking what it is you're investigating Victoria Deen for?"

"Oh, I don't mind you asking. But I can only tell you that the warrant is in relation to Title 26—tax evasion and general fraud."

"I figured you say something like that."

Two agents wheeled a flatbed cart, loaded with boxes, to a van parked on the curb.

PC turned back to Newman. "I'm happy Faudi's doing better. And if Victoria beats her murder rap, I'm glad you'll be waiting for her. That's... really all I had to say."

"Goodbye, Detective Donovan. I'm sure I'll be seeing you around."

That is not something you typically want to hear from an IRS agent.

PC raised her hand and waved as she walked down the long brick path to the parking lot. Once she got in her car, she started it and sat in the AC while she made a call.

"PC? What's up?"

"Hey, Drew. Hope I'm not disturbing you at work."

"No, not at all."

"Listen, I was wondering if you wanted to go to breakfast tomorrow."

"I would love to! But I can't. The Azalea Trail is back on."

"Oh. That's great."

"But if you want to do dinner tonight? Truffles!, perhaps? Seven-ish?"

"Sure. I'll see you later."

It was two weeks to the day that Victoria Deen confessed to the murder of Pete Danvers when PC drove Rose into Houston for her orthopedist appointment. She'd been a bit concerned for her mother, since she seemed to be having more pain and leaning more heavily on her cane.

After speaking with Dr. Thompson, he also seemed concerned, and sent Rose down the hall to be X-rayed. PC sat in the waiting room, trying to read a book on her phone. But every time the nurse opened the door to call a patient back, she jumped, hoping to hear her name. She'd read the same screen five times and didn't remember a word of it.

"Donovan?"

A nurse stood in the doorway with a clipboard.

PC scrambled to her feet. "Yes."

She followed the nurse, decked out in lavender scrubs, back to a different exam room from the one they'd started in. This one had a large screen on the wall. Rose sat there in a wheelchair, head down. PC sat in the seat closest to her.

A few interminable minutes later, Dr. Thompson came in.

"Miss Rose, I have some good news and some bad news."

He went to a computer at the side of the room and tapped on the keys. The screen flickered to life, then Rose's X-ray appeared, almost twice its actual size. He turned off the overhead light and walked over to the giant hip.

He pointed to the very bright new joint. "Miss Rose, it looks like your implant is still firmly set in the bone. That's the good news." He pointed to her hip. "The bad news is that the ball has pulled out of your hip socket. We don't have to replace anything or do any surgery, but we will have to knock you out to get it back into place."

"Oh, honey, when can you get that done? It's givin' me a lot of grief."

"I'm so sorry, Miss Rose. My nurse said there's a slot available next Tuesday. Does that work for you?

"If that's the first available."

"Alright. We will get you taken care of." Dr. Thompson looked up at PC. "You can confirm with the front desk, and they'll give you an instruction sheet. Do you have any questions?"

"How long will this take to heal?"

"She'll need to minimize her activity for at least the next thirty days. We'll have another look a month after the treatment and go from there."

"Okay. Thank you."

A nurse came in to wheel Rose along to the front desk. PC scheduled the procedure and picked up the instruction packet.

Looks like she'd be in Possumwood for another month. Maybe longer.

I guess there's always the re-enactment of the Battle of Mirabella Creek to look forward to.

When they got home and PC got Rose situated in her recliner, she stepped out onto the back porch to make a call.

"Hello?"

"Robin? It's PC. Is your niece still interested in renting the house?"

If you enjoyed this book, please consider leaving a review at your favorite book site. Reviews help other readers find and enjoy new books!

Other books by Holly Dey:

Manor of Death: The Possumwood Mysteries Book 1

Death on the Half Shell: The Possumwood Mysteries Book 2

Azalea Trail of Death: The Possumwood Mysteries Book 3

Death Re-Enacted: The Possumwood Mysteries Book 4

Death Rides a Bobcat: The Possumwood Mysteries Book 5

Key to Death: The Possumwood Mysteries Book 6

Death Curated: The Possumwood Mysteries Book 7

Pool of Death: The Possumwood Mysteries Book 8

All Death No Cattle: The Possumwood Mysteries Book 9

Death is Lager than Life: The Possumwood Mysteries Book 10

Art of Death: The Possumwood Mysteries Book 11

Little Town of Death-Lehem: The Possumwood Mysteries Book 12

Winter: Boxset Collection Books 1-3

Spring: Boxset Collection Books 4-6

Summer: Boxset Collection Books 7-9

Fall: Boxset Collection Books 10-12

All of the Possumwood Mysteries are available in

Large Print Editions